W9-ACR-880

When Old Men Die

Other Walker and Company Titles by Bill Crider

Featuring Truman Smith

Dead on the Island

Gator Kill

Featuring Professor Carl Burns

. . . *A Dangerous Thing*

When Old Men Die

A Truman Smith Mystery

Bill Crider

Walker and Company
New York

The Galveston of this novel, while it might bear a passing resemblance to the real thing, is purely a creation of memory and the imagination. The characters are, of course, entirely fictional.

First published in the United States of America in 1994
by Walker Publishing Company, Inc.

Published simultaneously in Canada by Thomas Allen & Son
Canada, Limited, Markham, Ontario

Library of Congress Cataloging-in-Publication Data
Crider, Bill, 1941–
When old men die / Bill Crider.
p. cm.
ISBN 0-8027-3195-3
I. Title.
PS3553.R497W48 1994
813'.54—dc20 94-15356
CIP

Printed in the United States of America
2 4 6 8 10 9 7 5 3 1

This book is for all the people who wrote the wonderful paperback original novels of the 1950s: William Campbell Gault, John D. MacDonald, Harry Whittington, Charles Williams, Jim Thompson, Gil Brewer, Day Keene, Stephen Marlowe, Michael Avallone, Ed McBain, Edward S. Aarons, J. M. Flynn, Milton K. Ozaki, Ed Lacy, Marvin H. Albert, Vin Packer, Bruno Fischer, Richard S. Prather, John McPartland, Peter Rabe, Robert Colby, Jonathan Craig, Ovid Demaris, and a host of others.

But why live if you don't have any illusions? At 69, what else is left? Ogden Nash said it:

> When old men die
> Nobody notices
> Except other old men.

—William Campbell Gault

When Old Men Die

▽

1

IN THE WINTER, the Gulf Coast Pier closes at five in the afternoon, so I figured I had another half hour to fish before I started gathering up my gear. I wouldn't have to worry about taking home any fish, since I hadn't even gotten a nibble. That was all right. I hadn't really expected to.

It was a beautiful January day on Galveston Island, a Saturday, fifty degrees and sunny, with a cloudless sky the color of that soft, light blue General Motors used on a lot of 1957 Buicks. But in spite of the nice weather, there was only one other person on the pier with me, a weather-beaten old man who'd probably been fishing somewhere along the seawall every day for the past thirty years.

The reason the pier was practically deserted was simple: The fish just weren't biting, in spite of the weather.

I got up off the bench where I'd been sitting for most of the afternoon reading a hard-back copy of *Look Homeward, Angel* while occasionally glancing at the tips of my rods in case there was any activity. I asked the old man if he wanted the rest of the bait shrimp in my blue plastic bucket, but he didn't. I poured them over the side of the pier and started reeling in one of my lines.

That was when I looked down at the entrance to the pier and saw Dino walking toward me. I might have been more surprised to see Jimmy Hoffa, but not much. Dino didn't get out often. And he especially didn't get out over the water. He might have seen the Gulf from his car window recently, but I would've bet he hadn't been on a pier in twenty years. A lot of the natives of the Island like to pretend that they never see the Gulf. Maybe they never do.

"Jesus Christ, Tru," Dino said when he got to my bench. "I had to pay three bucks just to walk out here to talk to you. Why don't you just fish off one of the rock jetties?"

"They don't have benches," I said.

"Yeah. And besides that, I'm missing *Geraldo*. Don't you ever watch TV?"

I stopped reeling and looked at him. "Not as much as you do."

I have my escapes from reality, and Dino has his. For a long time, his involved watching soap operas, but lately he's given them up for talk shows. He watches Sally, Phil, Geraldo, Jerry, Montel, Rolanda, Ricki, Vicki, and some others that I don't even know about. I think he even watches one in Spanish. But he's not watching as much as he used to. He gets out of the house more now.

I reeled in the rest of the line, took the beat-up shrimp off the hook, and tossed it in the Gulf. I wiped my hands on my sweatshirt and started reeling in the other line. Dino didn't mention TV again; he just sat on the bench and watched me.

"Not much luck, huh?" he said when I was finished.

"I threw them all back," I said. "I like to catch 'em, but I don't like to clean 'em."

"Bullshit," the old man said from the next bench. He was reeling in, too. "Ain't either one of us caught so much as a little old hardhead all day."

A truthful fisherman. That was all I needed. I ignored him and looked at the seawall to see if I could spot Dino's car. I did, and I thought I could see someone sitting behind the wheel.

"Did Evelyn drive you out here?" I asked.

Evelyn was the mother of Dino's daughter, Sharon. I'd helped him out with a problem involving Sharon a year or so back. Some people had gotten killed, which was too bad. They weren't very good people, maybe, but I'd done some of the killing, and I hadn't liked it. At least Dino and Evelyn had gotten together again as a result. And Sharon was doing better.

Dino pointed toward the seawall. "Evelyn's in the car. I sure as hell wasn't going to pay *six* bucks to talk to you."

I sat down beside him on the bench. "You could've waited until the pier closed."

"This is an emergency," he said, looking out over the Gulf.

The gray-green swells were gentle, barely whitecapping as they rolled to such beach as there was. There wasn't much, just a narrow strip of sand in front of the granite blocks that had been put in front of the seawall to keep the Gulf from undercutting it.

"You can tell him what it is," the old man said, gathering up his rods in one hand and his bucket in the other. "I won't be listenin'. I'm goin' home and fix me a big fish dinner. Tuna fish."

He laughed at his own little joke as he walked past us, and we watched him until he went through the gate at the snack bar.

"What's the emergency?" I asked then.

Dino looked back at the Gulf. "Outside Harry's disappeared," he said.

I hadn't met Outside Harry until a year or so ago when I'd come back to Galveston to find my sister, Jan. That was my specialty, finding people, but I hadn't found Jan. I never did, not exactly, but in the course of the looking I'd met Harry.

I'd known who he was ever since I was a kid. Practically everyone knew about him. He'd been on the Island for as long as most people could remember, though as far as anyone knew he didn't have a place to live. Harry had been homeless before homelessness had been cool, living out of the garbage cans behind grocery stores or on whatever money he could beg or borrow from the people he met, wearing several layers of clothing all year round and hauling his worldly goods in a shopping cart.

I'd found that Harry was a surprisingly good source of information about what went on in Galveston. He overheard a lot of things in his wanderings because no one paid him any attention. Often they didn't even notice him, and if they thought of him at all, they thought he was stupid. But they were wrong. He remembered most of what he heard and could repeat it with surprising accuracy.

"How do you know he's missing?" I asked Dino. "I didn't know you kept up with him."

Dino shrugged. "I don't. Not exactly."

The man who ran the snack bar and took up the admissions money was walking in our direction. I figured he wanted to go home. I didn't blame him. He hadn't made much money today.

"Let's go," I told Dino. "You can tell me the rest in the car."

Dino looked at his watch. "It's not five o'clock yet. I paid three bucks to sit here on this damn bench, and I'm going to get my money's worth."

"We'll be leaving in a minute," I told the man when he reached us. "We have a little business to discuss."

The man was tall and lanky, with a head of thick black hair. "Just as long as you're off by five," he said.

I promised him that we would be gone by then.

Dino waited until the man had walked back to the snack bar. "I been helping Harry out a little now and then ever since that business with Sharon."

That was Dino's way. You help him out, as Harry had done, though only in a small way, and Dino would help you out. That was the way it had been with Dino's uncles, back when Galveston was the leader in illegal gambling on the Gulf Coast and the uncles had practically been running the city, and that was the way it was with Dino now. It was the only way he knew.

"Helping him out how?" I asked.

Dino shrugged. "Giving him a handout now and then when he comes by the back door. Giving him a few bucks, too. Hell, Tru, he eats dog food. Did you know that?"

I nodded. "He likes it," I said.

Dino didn't appear convinced. "Yeah. Maybe. Anyway, he wouldn't take much from me. I just gave him as much as I could."

"And now he's missing?"

"That's right. He hasn't been by the house in a couple of weeks, which is longer than usual. So I asked around."

Dino hadn't been a part of the family business, but he still had connections. And while he'd tried to put the past behind him, the past is never behind you on the Island. To some people, the past is more important, and more real, than the present. So everyone remembered the uncles. When Dino "asked around," people responded.

"So what do you want me to do about it?" I asked, though I was afraid I already knew the answer.

Dino looked at me. "What the hell do you think I want you to do? I want you to find him."

I stood and gathered up my rods and bucket. "It's five o'clock," I said. "You can carry the book."

▽

2

THE THING IS, I don't try to find people anymore. I still have my P.I. license, but I gave up on finding people when I couldn't find Jan. Someone else did that, and they didn't find her, not really. They just found what was left.

I'd decided that if I couldn't even find my own sister, couldn't save her from her own death, then I couldn't find anybody, and for a while I was as bad as Dino, more or less hiding out from any real involvement with the world.

I painted houses for a few months, and then Dino asked me to find his daughter. I did that, and while it didn't turn out as well as I'd hoped, it did get me out of my self-absorption temporarily. Then someone hired me to find out who'd murdered an alligator. I took that job against my better judgment, but at least it hadn't involved finding anyone. And it had helped get me out of my shell a little more. I quit painting houses, and a month or so ago I'd gotten a real job, if you count working for a bail bondsman as a real job.

But I still don't try to find anyone. I'm not a bounty hunter. I just answer the phones and check up on people. If someone jumps bond, I do a little skip tracing by phone, but the heavy-duty stuff is up to someone else.

When we got to the seawall, I waved to Evelyn and waited until two Rollerbladers in helmets and pads swooshed by. Then I pitched the fishing rods and the bait bucket in the back of my Jeep, which was parked just in front of Dino's car, one of the last big Pontiacs they made before Detroit started downsizing. Dino didn't like small cars, and he hadn't bought a new one since the early eighties.

I, on the other hand, was driving what the former owner swore to me was a genuine World War II–vintage Jeep. I didn't really believe it was that old, though it certainly looked it.

"You need a new ride," Dino said. "You find Harry, I'll get you one."

"You're already doing enough for me," I told him. "You're letting me live in that house of yours."

"Yeah. Maybe I should start charging you some rent."

"It's not that great a house," I said, and it wasn't.

The house was old and run-down. It was located out past the western end of the seawall off Stewart Road, and it was nearly covered with bushes and vines. If you didn't know there was a house under there, you might think it was just a brier patch. And if we got a hurricane with a strong storm surge, God forbid, water would probably go right over the top of it.

"I fed your cat for you when you were trying to solve the murder of that alligator," Dino said.

I nodded. "He appreciated it. Me too." I started to climb in the Jeep.

Dino put a hand on my arm. "You can find Harry if you'll look. You're good at that stuff. I wish you'd stop this moping around."

"I'm not moping around. I fish, I go to work."

"Fishing. Yeah, right." He tossed *Look Homeward, Angel* into what was left of the passenger seat of the Jeep. "And you read books."

"Nothing wrong with reading," I said. "It improves the mind."

"Sure it does. So does helping people out, doing a little favor now and then."

"And I run," I added.

Dino glanced down at my right knee. "But not very fast," he said.

He should know. In college we both played football, and we were both pretty good. We weren't on the same team, though, and it was a collision between Dino's helmet and my knee that had left me with permanent ligament damage. I could still run, even if I couldn't go very fast, but I could never be sure when my right knee would collapse and send me sprawling. I had to take it easy when I jogged along the seawall or the beach.

"Look, Dino," I said, "Harry's probably around somewhere. Maybe he's just taking a few days off."

"Off what? It's not like he has a job or anything. If he was around, I'd know about it."

He was right, so I just shrugged and started to get in the Jeep. If I'd been faster I might have made it, but before I could get it started, Evelyn got out of Dino's car. She was a little older than Dino, but not too much. Her dark hair had hardly any gray in it, and it was tied back with a red ribbon.

She had to be careful getting out. There was a steady stream of pickup trucks and cars passing by on the wide street, their tires shushing along the pavement.

"Are you going to help him, Tru?" she asked. She was a head shorter than me, so she had to look up to catch my eyes.

I sighed and looked at the miniature golf course across the street. There was a giant turtle with a purple shell, something that looked like an anorexic dinosaur, and a small wrecked boat. There was no one playing golf that I could see.

I looked back down at Evelyn. "You know I don't like to do that kind of thing," I told her.

"Harry's your friend," she said.

Well, that wasn't really true. Harry was someone I knew, someone I talked to now and then, not a friend.

"Besides," Evelyn went on, "if you don't look for him, nobody will. Nobody cares what happens to an old man like that."

I should have said, "Why don't you and Dino look for him," but of course I didn't. Instead I said, "All right. You win. But I have to go in to work on Monday."

"So what does that mean?" Dino wanted to know.

"That means that I'll look for him tomorrow, but if he

doesn't turn up, I have a real job that I have to report to."

"This is a real job," Dino said. "I'll pay you. What're your rates?"

"I'm not doing it for money."

He reached in the back pocket of his cotton pants and pulled out a leather billfold. "You'll have expenses. Gas, food, maybe you'll even have to give somebody a few bucks for information."

He took out some bills and tried to hand them to me, but I didn't take them.

He was going to say something else, but we had to step into the street between the Jeep and the car to let a couple of joggers go by. There weren't as many people out as you might expect on such a nice day, but that was because it wasn't the tourist season. The BOIs, the people who were Born on the Island, were all at home. The exercisers had probably driven down from Houston, or maybe they were newcomers who worked at one of the hospitals or taught at the medical school.

Dino tried again to give me the money. I didn't take it that time either.

"It's just for one day," I said. "I won't need any gas, and I have to eat anyway."

He shoved the money into my hand. "You're a professional. Don't you want to be paid?"

He had a point there. I closed my hand on the money.

"Anyway," he said, "I don't want you to wait until tomorrow. I want you to start today."

"It won't be today much longer," I pointed out.

"I don't care about that. I want you to start now."

"You must like Harry a lot," I said.

"It's not that," Evelyn said. "He's an old man, and nobody cares what happens to him. Somebody should care."

I began to wonder just whose idea this whole thing was, but I knew better than to ask.

"All right," I said. "Can I go home and feed Nameless first?" Nameless is my cat.

Dino walked to his car and opened the front passenger door. He reached inside and came out with an unopened box of Tender Vittles.

"Seafood Supper," he said, holding it up for me to see. "We'll take care of the cat."

I shook my head. "You were pretty sure of me, weren't you?"

"You're a sucker for a sob story, all right," Dino said.

"I'm a sucker, period. Well, since the two of you have talked me into this, have you got any ideas about where I should begin?"

Dino grinned. "You're the detective."

"Great," I said. "Just great."

He punched me in the biceps with his free hand. "Don't be a sore loser."

I opened my hand and looked down at the bills. "I hope there's a lot of money here."

" 'The workman is worthy of his hire,' " Dino said. "That's what they used to tell me in Sunday School."

"You never went to Sunday School in your life."

"Maybe I heard it on Postoffice Street, then."

"Hush, Dino," Evelyn said.

She probably didn't like to be reminded of Postoffice Street, which is where Galveston's red light district was located for a long, long time. Evelyn knew. She had worked there.

She didn't work there now, however. She was a receptionist in the Ashbell Smith Building, built in 1890 and better known as Old Red, the first building of the Texas Medical College, now The University of Texas Medical Branch. She didn't want anyone there to know about her past, and I didn't blame her.

"Well," Dino said, "I heard it somewhere. It doesn't make any difference where it was. And there's plenty of money there."

"I know there is," I said. "It's just that there's not a whole lot to go on here. I don't even have a place to start."

"We're not worried about that," Dino told me. "Like I said, you're a professional. You'll think of something."

I shoved the money into the pocket of my loose-fitting jeans. "You have a lot more faith in me than I have in myself."

Dino tossed the box of Tender Vittles in the air and caught it. "That wouldn't take much, would it?" he asked.

"No," I said. "It wouldn't take a whole lot."

"I didn't think so," he said. "And that's another reason why you should take the job."

Maybe he had a point there. But I didn't really think so.

▽

3

ACTUALLY, THINGS WEREN'T as bad as I'd tried to make them seem to Dino. There was somewhere to start, even when you were looking for a street person like Harry. There was always somewhere to start.

Or if not, there was some*one* to start with. At least there was if I could find him. His name was Ro-Jo, and to my surprise, I located him in less than a minute.

I said good-bye to Evelyn and Dino, got in the Jeep, and drove east on Seawall Boulevard. I spotted Ro-Jo after I'd gone about twenty blocks. He was on the concrete walkway leading to the 61st Street Pier. His grocery cart, never out of his sight, was beside him. There was no one fishing on that pier, either, so Ro-Jo wasn't in anyone's way.

I hadn't expected to find him so easily. He's usually scrounging in the Dumpsters behind Kroger or Randall's, or maybe one of the fast-food places, hoping that someone's thrown out something edible. It wouldn't have to be something I'd consider edible. Ro-Jo was like Harry. They had standards that were a little different from mine.

I parked the Jeep and climbed out. Ro-Jo hadn't spotted me yet, so I watched him for a minute. Him and the cats.

All along the seawall, on the beach side, there are cats living in the rocks. I suspected that Ro-Jo had eaten some tuna fish or maybe even cat food that day, or some day recent enough for the smell to still be in his clothing. The cats swirled around him as he tried to tie the bottoms of his camouflage pants to his ankles as tightly as he could with a frayed piece of toweling.

"Hey, Ro-Jo," I called when he was finished. "Are those your cats?"

Ro-Jo looked up. I think that his hair had once been red and that he'd been called *Rojo*, which is Spanish for red if you pronounce the *j* like an *h*. But no one called him that anymore, and the new pronunciation didn't matter because his hair was no longer red. It was tangled, matted, and greasy, and maybe you could call it auburn if you were feeling poetic.

His camouflage suit looked fairly new, but the toweling that now tied it to his ankles and wrists looked older than I am, as did the rusty grocery cart that he had piled high with his worldly possessions, all of which were packed in black garbage bags and covered with a clear plastic drop cloth.

"What're you tying down for?" I asked him, walking down to where he stood.

"Gonna get cold tonight, man." His beard and mustache were so thick that I could hardly see his mouth as he spoke. "Gotta keep that frigid air outta my sleeves and britches' legs."

I looked around at the cats rubbing against his ankles and swarming around both of us now, gray tabby cats, calico cats, black cats, any kind of motley cat you could think of. I wondered if Nameless had lived along the seawall before he adopted me.

"Nice pets," I said.

"They aren't mine, man. I don't even like cats."

He was wearing a pair of worn Nike cross trainers, and to prove his point he used the toe of one to shove aside a little calico.

"If you don't like them, you could kick harder than that."

"Hey, man, I didn't kick her. I don't kick animals, even if they bother me, which these don't. I might not like 'em, but they keep down the rats. And besides, these cats got enough trouble without me kickin' 'em."

"What kind of trouble?"

"They live in these rocks here," he said, pointing along the seawall. "But when the tide comes in, what happens?"

"It covers the rocks," I said.

Ro-Jo looked surprised that I'd gotten the answer, but I was a detective, after all. I could figure out stuff like that.

Ro-Jo bobbed his head. "Right, man. The tide comes in and covers the rocks, and these cats got no place to go except across those four lanes of traffic there." He gestured in the direction of the street. "Lots of mashed cats, man."

While we were talking, a white pickup stopped in front of my Jeep and a man got out. He took a bucket from the pickup bed and started stirring something in it with a stick.

The cats deserted me and Ro-Jo instantly and teemed around the man from the pickup.

"What's going on?" I asked Ro-Jo.

"Feeding time, man."

While we watched, the man put cat food out on the rocks. The cats gulped it greedily. Some seagulls appeared out of nowhere and swooped down to check out the food, but not close enough for the cats to grab them.

"Who's the guy?" I asked.

"I don't know, man. All I know is, he feeds the cats."

Everyone was doing favors these days. Some good Samaritan was even feeding the seawall cats. I guessed the least I could do was ask a few questions about Outside Harry. I figured that if anyone had seen him, Ro-Jo would be the one. I'd seen them together on the streets a couple of times.

"I don't know where he is, man," Ro-Jo said when I asked. "I ain't seen that old dude in a couple weeks. Maybe more than that. Where's he hangin' out, anyhow?"

"That's what I wanted you to tell me," I reminded him.

"Oh. Yeah. Right. Well, I don't know."

"You have a place you go when it gets cold?"

He narrowed his eyes, which were nearly as hard to see as his mouth, what with the hair hanging out from under the old Astros cap he wore and growing high on his cheeks.

"What you want to know that for, man?"

"I'm not planning to sneak in and rob you in the middle of the night," I told him. "I just thought Harry might have a place like that, and I wondered if you knew where it was."

"Maybe," he said, watching the man who had fed the cats get into his truck and leave. "Maybe not."

Well, what could I expect? I pulled out my billfold and gave him a ten.

It disappeared inside the camouflage suit. "You know that old building down on East Beach by those condos? Looks like some kinda old pump station or something?"

"I know it."

It wasn't a pump station, though, whatever that was. I thought it used to be some kind of marine laboratory.

"Harry said something about it to me once," Ro-Jo went on. "It's not much of a place, though. There's better."

"Where?"

He stuck out a hand.

What the hell, I thought. It was Dino's money.

Actually, it wasn't, not that specific money. It was mine. All the bills Dino had given me were bigger than any I had, but I wasn't giving Ro-Jo any of those. I handed him another ten. That left me one more of my own.

This bill disappeared faster than the first one had. "There's The Island Retreat," Ro-Jo said.

The Island Retreat was a memory of Galveston's heyday, when Dino's uncles were in power, and when there was as much gambling going on right there on the Island as there was in Las Vegas. The Retreat was supposed to be a restaurant, and food was actually served there, but gambling was the main attraction.

The Texas Rangers raided The Retreat with regularity, but they never found a thing. The causeway in those days featured a drawbridge, and somehow the Rangers were always getting delayed on their way to the Island. By the time they arrived, there was no sign of any gambling apparatus.

Once, or so I'd heard, they got by the watchers and the drawbridge and came right into The Retreat, but the pier was so long, and the uncles so skilled in delaying tactics—talking, whining, pleading, demanding warrants—that by the time the Rangers reached the room at the end of the pier where the gambling went on, there was nothing to be seen but a group of happy diners eating at tables covered with sparkling white cloths.

Storms had shortened the pier, but a lot of the old building was still there, boarded up and covered with FOR SALE signs. It might be a good place to get out of the cold, but it was right on the busiest part of the seawall, and the door had certainly appeared to be locked securely every time I glanced at it in passing.

I asked Ro-Jo how anyone could get inside.

"You have to wait till after dark," he said.

"The street's pretty well lighted along there," I said.

"I didn't say anything about going in by the front door, man."

"All right. So how do you get in?"

Ro-Jo didn't say anything. He looked over my shoulder at the sky. I turned and looked too. The blue had turned dark, and there were a few low clouds turned orange and pink by the setting sun. I looked back at Ro-Jo. He was rubbing his fingers together, so I gave him my last ten.

"You gotta climb up the pier, man," he said after making the bill vanish. "Third pole on the west side. There's a hole in the floor you can get through if you know where it is."

He stopped and looked at me.

"I don't have any more money," I said. "You've got it all already, so you might as well tell me."

He did. It would involve a little wading, but not much.

"You mean Harry can climb the pier?" I said. "He looks too old for that."

Ro-Jo shrugged. "Hey, man, when you're lookin' for a warm place to sleep, you can do a lot of things."

Maybe he was right. I supposed that if Harry could do it, I could. If Dino had still owned the building, I could just have asked for a key, but the uncles had lost control of most of their real estate before they died, and I was sure that Dino wasn't the owner of The Retreat. He probably didn't even know who was.

"Thanks for your help, Ro-Jo," I said. "I'll see you around."

"Yeah, you might. Why're you lookin' for Harry, anyhow?"

I was already on my way to the Jeep. "Somebody wants to know where he is," I said over my shoulder.

"I know that, man. I just wondered why *you* were lookin'."

I stopped and turned back at Ro-Jo. "You know somebody's looking for Harry?"

"Sure, man. I've made more bread this week than in the last ten years."

"Someone else gave you money to tell them about Harry?"

"That's what I've been saying. Takes you a while to catch on, doesn't it?"

"Who was it?"

"I don't know man, just some guy."

"What did he look like?"

Ro-Jo looked at me with what might have been contempt. It was nearly impossible to see his expression.

"I don't know, man. I don't give a damn what people look like."

He was probably telling the truth. I didn't press him on it.

"Did you tell him the same thing you've told me?" I asked.

"Hell, no, man. I didn't know *him*. I don't tell anybody the truth unless I know 'em."

"But you're telling me the truth?"

"Sure, man. I know you, and Harry knows you. He says you're all right for a guy who lives in a house."

"It's not much of a house," I said.

Ro-Jo opened his arms. "More than I got. You gonna look for Harry?"

"I'm supposed to."

"Well, if you find him, tell him Ro-Jo says 'hey.' "

I promised that I would.

▽

4

I DIDN'T WANT to try The Island Retreat, not until well after dark and much later in the evening. Someone was sure to see me if I did.

That left the old concrete building that Ro-Jo had mentioned, so I headed in that direction. When I came to the more populated area of the seawall, I glanced over to my right as I passed one of the gift shops that extended out over the Gulf on its own pier. Only a few yards farther on was The Island Retreat. Just as I remembered, the doors were securely fastened, the windows boarded up. I kept on driving.

After you pass Stewart Beach, there's not much to see. Suddenly the seawall is on your left, and you're driving practically at sea level.

There's very little development on that end of the Island, except for two high-rise condos that are practically on the beach, a testament to man's undying faith that the next big storm, which is certainly going to come some day, will be perfectly harmless, no more than a passing breeze that might ruffle a few palm branches or tear the blossoms off the oleanders that grow along the esplanade on Broadway.

It's nice to be optimistic, but I'd put my money on that part of the beach being as clean the day after the storm as if it had been swept by a broom. Of course, I've been wrong before.

At the far end of the Island was Appfel Park, which at the right time of the year would be covered with tourists and day-trippers from Houston. There probably wouldn't be many people there now, especially at this time of day. After passing Appfel Park, you came to Bolivar Roads; there was no more Island left.

The place I was looking for was on the town side of East Beach and within sight of the high-rise condos, but then so is everything else on that end of the Island.

The building was about a hundred yards off the street, right on the edge of a lagoon. There was an oyster shell road running down toward it through the tall sea oats, but the road was blocked by a rusty gate. There was a sign hanging on the gate. The sign was white with black letters and spotted with rust. It said:

KEEP OUT
U. S. GOVERNMENT PROPERTY
TRESPASSERS WILL BE PROSECUTED

If I went past the gates, would I be considered a trespasser? I didn't see how. After all, the government is the people, isn't it? And I was one of the people. So this was *my* property, wasn't it? My tax dollars at work, and all that.

I had a strong feeling that if I were caught, no judge in the country would buy that line of reasoning, but I didn't think I'd be caught. There certainly wouldn't be a guard. No one cared about that crumbling old hunk of concrete. Someone had probably put the sign up because a lawyer had given a speech about liability in case of accident, but I didn't intend to hurt myself and sue.

I looked around for a place to park the Jeep. Parking right in front of the gate seemed a little too obvious. Someone was sure to see the Jeep and wonder what it was doing there. I could have driven to one of the condos, but their parking places were probably guarded a lot more tightly than this building was.

There was a paved road leading down to the condos located not too far from the old lab building, and just off the road there was a small pool. Ruts led through the sea oats to the pool, where someone had driven down to it, maybe to cast a net for bait.

There was no gate across these ruts, so I could drive down to the pool and leave the Jeep, hoping that anyone who saw the Jeep would assume that a fisherman was somewhere around, even if I wasn't in sight. It was nearly dark now, and I didn't think anyone would see the Jeep down there anyway.

A big heron flew up off the pool when I drove up and sailed off gracefully, looking startlingly white against the darkening sky. I sat and watched him for a minute before taking my Mag-Lite from under the passenger seat and getting out of the Jeep.

As I walked through the nearly head-high sea oats toward where I hoped Harry was hiding out, I wondered who besides me was looking for him.

And I wondered why.

I also wondered if Dino had leveled with me. If he'd been lying, it wouldn't have been the first time. When he'd asked me to look for Sharon, he'd told me that she was the daughter of "a friend." Which was true, if you considered that Evelyn was his friend. Still, he should have told me that Sharon was his daughter as well. Eventually he did, of course, but he'd held back in the beginning.

It was a shame that a man couldn't trust even an old friend to be truthful.

Harry must have known someone was looking for him. That was no doubt why he had disappeared in the first place. I just couldn't imagine what anyone would want with him. He didn't have any money, at least not that I knew about. For that matter, he didn't have anything, not unless he'd found something in the Dumpsters or in the alleys. If he'd done that, he hadn't told Ro-Jo about it.

Or maybe he had. Maybe Ro-Jo had taken it from him and quietly disposed of him. That was possible, but not very likely. Ro-Jo was a peaceable sort. He would take money from me for information, but he wasn't aggressive. He didn't like to confront people. He wouldn't even kick a cat.

The oats slapped against my jeans, and I could hear the gentle sound of the surf on the beach. It was soothing and peaceful, a little like listening to a New Age relaxation tape.

There was still the faint glow of the sunset in the west, but the sky overhead was dark and a few stars were breaking through. The dark gray bulk of the building loomed high on its concrete stilts in front of me.

When I reached it, I could see what Ro-Jo meant when he'd said it wasn't much of a place. Whatever purpose the building had once served, it was now only a skeleton. There was enough light for me to see that the outside walls were solid, but the windows had quite a few missing panes, and a lot of the ones that weren't missing were broken. There were a couple of tall antennas sticking up from the roof, but I suspected that there was no receiving or sending equipment inside.

The place certainly didn't look very inviting, but maybe that was just the kind of place Harry would look for if he wanted to hole up from the weather. He probably wouldn't have much company.

I turned on the flashlight and shined it around the stilts. Most of them were in the shallow water of the lagoon, though a couple in front were on relatively dry land. There was no sign of Harry's shopping cart, but he would probably have stowed that elsewhere. Maybe he had even managed to get it inside the building somehow.

On the side of the building there was a rickety wooden stairway leading up. The salty air had just about rotted it away, and I wondered if it would hold my weight or if one of the steps would crumble away to nothing when I put my foot on it. Or maybe it would just break in two.

There was one way to find out. I squished over to the stairs and started climbing.

I got up them with no trouble at all. They were still solid, no matter how bad they looked, but they squealed when I put my weight on them. If Harry was there, he would know I was coming.

Or he would know that someone was coming. I thought I'd better tell him so he wouldn't try to hide and make it harder for me to find him.

"Harry!" I said. "Are you up there? This is Truman Smith."

There was no answer, but I thought I heard something scratching around on the concrete floor. It could have been Harry, or it could have been a cat. It could have been nearly anything.

"Harry? You up there?"

Still no answer, but I was beginning to feel a little uneasy. Maybe Harry wasn't there, but maybe whoever else was looking for him was. I was sorry I'd ever let Dino and Evelyn talk me into this, but I kept on climbing the stairs.

When I got to the top, I called out again. "Harry?"

My own voice echoed back off a concrete wall, but aside from that there was no sound at all except the surf and the wind in the sea oats. Somewhere along the beach a car horn honked.

I went inside the building and found myself standing in a large open room with two doors leading into the rest of the building. There was some trash over in one corner, and I shined the flashlight on it: some aluminum soft drink cans, a few old newspapers, and what looked like some flat tins that might have held tuna or cat food. Harry's kind of meal. Maybe he was there after all. I turned off the flashlight.

"Harry?" I said.

There was a soft scratching from somewhere farther inside the building. I walked to the far end and went through one of the doors.

The next room was very dark, and there was no one in there, either. There was also no trash on the floor. I crossed it and went through another door.

As soon as I stepped through there was a soft *pop* and

sparks jumped from the side of the doorway near my head. A sliver of concrete hit me in the ear.

I dived forward and hit the floor, sliding along it, scraping my hands and tearing a hole in the knee of my jeans. I felt a sharp pain in my right knee, which meant that the old football injury hadn't taken the fall too well. Just another thing to thank Dino for the next time I saw him. Assuming that I ever saw him again.

The next shot went over my head and hit the wall behind me.

The good news was that I still had my flashlight, which might have been fine if there had been any use for it.

There was even more good news. It was extremely dark in the room where I was lying, and I was wearing a gray sweatshirt and blue jeans, which would make me very hard to see.

But that was pretty much the end of the good news. The bad news was that I was trapped.

I was also scared. I didn't like being shot at. It made my palms sweat, and it gave me a funny feeling in the pit of my stomach. It's pretty depressing to know that someone is trying to kill you and that there's not much you can do about it.

I might have felt a little better about things if I'd been carrying a pistol of my own, but I wasn't. So there wasn't much I could do except lie there on the cold concrete floor and sweat. And wait.

▽

5

IT MIGHT COME as a surprise to a lot of people to know that I wasn't carrying a handgun, but contrary to popular belief, not everyone in Texas goes around armed to the teeth.

In fact, there are laws against that sort of thing, though the state legislature is beginning to make an effort to change that. Sometimes it seems that there are members of that august body who would like to see the citizens all walking down the streets with Colt's Peacemakers in holsters strapped around their waists.

But until that day comes, it's illegal to carry a pistol. You can own one, or a hundred for that matter, which is fairly interesting, since in Texas owning six or more devices defined as "sexual apparatus" is a serious criminal offense.

Ever hear of anyone being killed with a dildo? OK, maybe it's possible, but as far as I know I never heard of a drive-by dildoing.

At any rate, in Texas you can own as many pistols as you please, and you can carry a pistol in your car as long as you keep it locked in the trunk or the glove compartment. But it's illegal to take it out of the car and carry it unless you're on your own property.

So, being a law-abiding citizen, I didn't have a pistol. I hadn't thought I'd need one.

I didn't even have a dildo.

I had a flashlight, and maybe I could do something with that, after all. I wondered if it would be a good idea to try explaining the Texas firearms laws to whoever was shooting at me before I tried the thing with the flashlight.

Probably not.

There was another *pop* and another chunk of concrete chip flew out of the wall. This *pop* was louder. The silencer was tearing apart.

Whoever was doing the shooting was in the next room, and he was shooting through what must once have been a window. But it was so dark that I couldn't see a thing, not even a shadow. Just a muzzle flash.

The shooter couldn't see me either, though. He kept shooting high, but I was afraid that sooner or later he'd catch on and aim lower. That made me sweat a little harder. I had to do something before I got shot, and I had to do it now.

The flashlight was all I had, so I turned it on and rolled it across the floor.

There were three quick shots, two of them scoring the floor; the third one glanced off the flashlight and sent it spinning crazily. It kept right on shining, though, which just goes to show that it pays to buy good equipment. That anodized aluminum is good stuff.

By the third shot I was on my feet and lurching toward the door. I should have been moving more smoothly, but I was doing the best I could, considering that my knee was threatening to collapse under me at every step.

I told myself that I should have been lurching away from the shooter. That would have been the smart thing, especially since my stomach was still in knots, but there was something about being shot at that made me mad. And being mad made me stupid.

I went through a doorway into the next room, but no one was there. I could hear footsteps echoing off the concrete walls as someone ran through the building. They weren't my footsteps. I was wearing an old pair of Nike Air Spans with rubber soles.

I didn't know why the shooter was running. Maybe he thought I had a weapon after all. Maybe he was out of cartridges.

I heard noises coming from the room next to me and realized that he'd doubled back. I didn't know anything about the arrangement of the rooms, but I knew that there was only one stairway. If I just retraced my steps, maybe I could beat him to it.

I almost did. I came into the room a little behind him, but I didn't get much of a look at him. It was too dark, and he was nothing more than a vague, bulky shape.

I made a grab for him, and just about then my knee went out. As I was falling, I got a handful of his shirt, nearly ripping it off his back.

"Sonofabitch," he said.

Then he whirled around and hit me in the face with his pistol.

I was already down, and he was off balance, so he didn't hit me as hard as he might have. I felt the skin on my cheek tear, though, and for just a second I couldn't hear, see, or feel anything at all.

By the time I shook my head to clear it and tried to stand up, the shooter was clattering down the stairway.

Just to prove that I hadn't learned anything from getting my face bashed, I tried to follow him. Luckily, I got most of the way down before the knee went again, so I didn't have far to fall.

The ground was soft, but I was a little slower getting up that time, and when I did, the shooter was gone. I didn't know which direction he'd taken, and he was out of sight in the waving sea oats. There was no sound of splashing from the lagoon, so he'd probably gone around the end. It wasn't a long way. Or he could be lying out there in the oats, waiting for me.

I stood there for a while leaning on the stair rail, hoping that a car would start up somewhere and give me a clue, but nothing happened.

I touched my fingers to my face. I was still bleeding, but not much. There was a loose flap of skin, but nothing that would need stitching up.

A few cars passed by on the road above me, but that was all. There were lights on in a lot of the condo windows, and I wondered if anyone down there had heard the shots. There wasn't much chance of that.

After about fifteen minutes, I went back up the stairs. This time my knee held up, but I was going pretty slowly. My flashlight was still shining, but the aluminum casing was severely dented.

No one bothered me while I looked in all the rooms of the old building.

I found a few more signs that Harry, or someone, might have stayed there, but it was hard to say just how recently that had been. The flat tins had held tuna, all right, and there was a fleck or two of meat left in them, but it was hard and dry.

In another room there were some more old newspapers that someone might have used to stuff in his clothes for warmth, but there was no way of knowing for sure if they'd been used for that purpose.

And that was all I ferreted out. Not even a rock, a leaf, or an unfound door, as Thomas Wolfe might have put it. I wondered if anyone besides me even read Thomas Wolfe anymore.

I left the building and went back to the Jeep and sat for a minute, resting my forearms on the wheel and wondering whether I should try looking at The Island Retreat. It didn't take me long to decide that that wasn't a good idea. I'd already been shot at once, and I wasn't going to take a chance on its happening again. Besides, my knee was hurting and my head was throbbing.

I decided that I'd go home and try to get some sleep. Tomorrow I'd have a little talk with Dino.

▽

6

IT HAD GOTTEN a lot cooler while I was chasing around, though I hadn't noticed it until I started driving the Jeep. The old vehicle had one real disadvantage: it was completely open, so there was no protection from the weather. If I folded down the windshield, there would be nothing at all between me and the wind.

There was a thin crescent of moon now, and the stars were icy in the black sky. The temperature must have dropped at least fifteen or twenty degrees in the last hour. No wonder Ro-Jo had been tying down his pants' legs. At least the cold wind took my mind off being shot at.

I had to drive practically the length of the Island to get home, and by the time I got to the house I was thoroughly chilled. I parked the Jeep and looked around for Nameless. He wasn't in sight, and he didn't come when I called. Probably out terrorizing the lizards that lived in the bushes.

I got my copy of *Look Homeward, Angel* out of the passenger seat and started inside. There was a food bowl by the front door with a few Tender Vittles still in it, so I supposed that Dino had been here.

I went in and lit the gas heaters in the bedroom and bathroom. Then I checked my face in the bathroom mirror. The cut wasn't deep, and it looked worse than it was. I found a little pair of fingernail scissors, cut off the flap of skin, and put some alcohol on the place. I had to grit my teeth to keep from yelling. Then I covered it with a bandage and took a couple of ibuprofen for my headache. The sliver of concrete had cut a little place on my ear, but it didn't need a bandage. I looked at my knee through the rip in my jeans. The skin was abraded but not broken, and I decided against alcohol. I'd had enough pain for one night.

I went into the kitchen. I was hungry, but I don't keep much to eat around the place. I'm not a cook, and I usually just eat at a restaurant. Tonight I settled for a peanut butter sandwich with apricot jelly. I made it on whole wheat bread to keep it healthy.

I poured a glass of Big Red to wash the peanut butter down, and went into the bedroom, which is where most of my furniture is. I have a sprung recliner, a bed, a dresser, and a bookcase. I also have a CD player.

The disc player was already loaded with a two-CD set by The Drifters, a disc by Clyde McPhatter, and two by the Coasters. I turned on the amp, set the player to shuffle all the discs, and turned on the power.

For a long time I'd resisted buying a CD player, but then I'd discovered that record companies were raiding their vaults and putting everything they had on disc. As soon as I discovered that the disc of The Drifters' "Let the Boogie-Woogie Roll" had several more tracks on it than the tape did, I was a goner.

The Coasters broke into "Wake Me, Shake Me," and I started feeling better almost immediately. I sat in the recliner and ate my sandwich and listened.

After a couple of songs, I started thinking about what had happened. The more I thought about it, the more it bothered me. I didn't like being in the dark about what was going on, and I *really* didn't like being shot at.

The question I most wanted an answer to was why someone would shoot at me.

Of course it could have been that the U. S. Government was really serious about keeping trespassers out of their building or out of their lagoon. There was about as much chance of that, I thought, as of the Houston Oilers going to the Super Bowl within my lifetime.

There really weren't many other possibilities. The most obvious was that someone didn't want me to find Harry, which brought me back to another question I would have liked to have an answer for. Why was someone else looking for Harry?

I drank my Big Red and thought about phoning Dino, but he could wait until tomorrow when I'd be feeling stronger. If he'd set me up, I was going to try beating the hell out of him. It wouldn't be easy. I was in pretty good shape from jogging, but that mostly helped my legs. Dino was the one who pumped iron and had arms that looked as if they could bend a tire tool. Besides, I had a feeling that deep down inside he was a lot meaner than I was.

Of course it didn't have to be Dino who'd set me up. Ro-Jo had said that he hadn't told the other person looking for Harry the same things he'd told me. But someone had been waiting in the old building. How had he known to go there unless Ro-Jo had told him? I was going to have to talk to Ro-Jo again, too, if I could find him. For some reason I didn't think it would be as easy as it had been the last time.

Clyde McPhatter was singing about the treasure of love when I heard Nameless scratching on the front screen door. I went to open it and let him in.

He's big and yellowish orange, with gray-green eyes. He took his time about entering. He looked up at me as if to ask where I'd been all evening, then stretched and gawked and looked behind him before stepping daintily through the door. After that he quickly picked up the pace, tearing through the nearly bare living room like a rocket, speeding through the bedroom door, and then jumping on the bed, where he proceeded to lick his fur in that self-satisfied way cats have.

I followed him into the bedroom. "Is the music all right?" I asked him. It was The Coasters again. "Little Egypt."

Nameless didn't even bother looking at me. He just kept licking himself. He was purring, however, so I assumed that he approved. Then he stuck out one of his back legs, spread his toes, and started biting between them. I had no idea what that meant.

I sat back in my chair. It was going to be harder to find Harry than I'd first thought, and I wanted to do it even less than I had before.

It was going to be harder because it seemed certain that Harry wasn't just looking for a warm place to sleep like I'd first thought. He knew that someone was after him, and he had gone into hiding.

I wanted to find him even less than before, because now there was a kind of urgency to the hunt, and I didn't want to fail him the way I'd failed Jan.

And I *had* failed her, and myself, no matter how many times I told myself that I hadn't, and no matter how many times others told me the same thing.

The way I saw it, if I had come back to the Island in time, she wouldn't be dead. I was convinced that it was as simple as that.

Her remains were found in a field not far off the interstate quite a while after I came back, and despite the medical examiner's estimate that her death had occurred long before my return, I would always feel that there was something I could have done, something I *should* have done. Whatever it had been, I hadn't done it. I wasn't even the one who eventually found her.

And now Harry had gone missing. It wasn't my fault; it didn't have anything at all to do with me. So why was I already feeling guilty?

I thought it might be a good idea to try beating the hell out of Dino even if he hadn't tried to set me up. I would never have gotten involved in this mess if it hadn't been for him, and there was no way out of it now. I was going to have to try to find Harry. I was going to have to try to keep him from winding up the way Jan had.

"What are we going to do about it?" I asked Nameless.

He didn't answer, having curled up and gone to sleep with his tail over his nose. Obviously, Harry's plight didn't bother him in the least. I wished that I could have taken things that calmly.

I got out of the chair and took a shower, trying not to get any water on my bandage. Then I went back into the bedroom and turned off the CD player as soon as The Drifters finished singing "Money Honey." I went over to the bed and shoved Nameless out of the way. He woke up and looked at me without resentment. After a little more licking, he settled down on the other side of the bed.

He was asleep long before I was.

▽

7

THE SKY WAS covered with clouds the next morning, and the low, gray overcast fit my mood perfectly. I fed Nameless in the kitchen, then let him outside. He charged into the brush, and I brought in the paper.

My headache was gone, so I put on a pair of shorts and a top and went out for a run. I pulled the bandage off to let the air get to the cut on my face. The sweat stung it a little, but otherwise it was a lot better. Even my knee held up better than I'd expected.

The house where I lived was out past the developed part of the Island, and though the development started again a little farther down the road, my nearest neighbors lived in places with rolls of hay or old car bodies in the yard. I wondered what the people who lived in the fancy condos and houses on stilts thought about that. I don't suppose it worried them much. In a few years the run-down old houses would be gone, replaced by more fashionable residences. Most likely no one would miss the old places but me. I thought they added a little character to the neighborhood.

After a couple of miles I turned back. Nameless wasn't around, and I didn't waste any time looking for him. I went inside and took a shower. For breakfast I had some Frosted Mini-Wheats while I went through the paper. There wasn't much of interest outside the comics. When I'd read all I wanted to read, I called Dino.

"What'd you find out?" he asked.

"More than I thought I would. Are you going to be at home for a while?"

"Yeah. I'm just reading the Sunday funnies. 'Calvin and Hobbes' cracks me up. You read that one?"

"I read them all except 'Rex Morgan,' " I said.

"Hey, you oughta give that one a try. It deals with some serious stuff."

"So do I. I'll be over in a few minutes."

I had on a clean sweatshirt and the jeans I'd worn the day before. With the ripped knee, the jeans were much more fashionable than they had been. Before I left, I slipped on an old corduroy jacket. If there was no sun, the day would be colder than the one before.

Dino's house was in a neighborhood not far from Moody Gardens, along with a lot of other brick houses that wouldn't have looked out of place in one of the older neighborhoods of Waco. If I hadn't known the Gulf was just a short distance away, I'd have thought I was in Central Texas. Lots of the Island's older residents like it that way; they don't want anything to remind them that they're sitting at sea level, just a stone's throw from the water.

"Hey, Tru," Dino said when he met me at the door. "Come on in. I got some Big Red in the refrigerator, but I bet even you can't drink that stuff this early in the morning."

It was nearly ten o'clock, which wasn't early except to people like Dino, who really didn't get going until noon. I told him I could drink a glass of Big Red.

I didn't mention that I'd thought about beating the hell out of him. It hadn't seemed like such a good idea last night, and in the light of day it seemed even worse.

Dino went into the kitchen to get the Big Red. There had been a time when he'd had someone to do that sort of thing for him, but that friendship had come to a bad end. I thought about Ray and what had happened to him. I hoped nothing like that was going to happen again.

I sat on the sturdy floral sofa that looked as if it had been in the house for forty years, which it probably had, like nearly all of Dino's furniture. The room hadn't changed much at all since I'd last been there except for a Super Nintendo game system that was now hooked up to the huge TV set. The only modern stuff was the electronic equipment.

On an end table by the couch there was a lamp that provided the only light in the room. The heavy curtains on the windows were drawn to keep out the light. And maybe to keep out any reminders of the outside world as well.

Dino came back in a few minutes. He had the Big Red in a glass with some ice cubes. He had something brown for himself, but I didn't ask what.

"Play-off games this afternoon," he said, handing me my drink and pointing to the TV set. "You think the Cowboys will win again?"

I said I didn't know and took a sip of the drink. I wasn't a Cowboy fan.

Dino sat on the other end of the couch. "You said you found something out. Are you gonna tell me what?" He looked at me as if noticing the scratch on my face for the first time. "And what happened to you?"

The Big Red was as sweet as bubble gum. "Tell me again why you wanted me to find Harry," I said.

Dino moved three or four remotes out of the way and set his drink on the Duncan Phyfe coffee table that stood in front of the couch.

"I already told you that," he said. "I've sort of been helping him out. He's a friend, I guess you could say, and I'm worried about him."

"Sure you are."

He tried to look hurt. "You sayin' I can't have a friend like Harry?"

I took another drink of Big Red. "I'm not saying that. I'm

just wondering if there's anything you didn't tell me. Anything that I might need to know."

He furrowed his brow. "You think I left something out?"

"That's what I'd like to know," I said, and then I told him what I'd learned from Ro-Jo and what had happened later on.

"Jesus, Tru. I'm sorry somebody took a shot at you. And I'm sorry you got hit in the face. But I didn't have anything to do with it. I hope you didn't think I was holding out on you. You didn't think that, did you?"

"It crossed my mind."

"I thought you knew me better than that."

"That's the trouble," I said. "I know you too well."

Dino laughed, but it wasn't very convincing. "Well, I was telling you the truth. If there's someone looking for Harry besides you, I don't know about it. Anyway, how can you be sure that you didn't just scare some other street person who was looking for a place to get out of the wind?"

I hadn't considered that, but now that he'd brought it up I didn't really think it was a possibility. It was too much of a coincidence to think that someone besides Harry would be staying in the old marine lab, especially someone who'd open fire on me. I don't believe in coincidences like that.

"Maybe I did scare somebody," I said. "But it wasn't a street person. I've got another question for you."

"Shoot."

"Poor choice of words," I told him.

"Sorry. Ask away."

"Who owns The Island Retreat?"

Dino looked over at his TV as if he wished the play-off game had already started.

"I don't know," he said. "I lost track of who owned all those places a long time ago."

"There's a realtor's sign on it."

"That doesn't tell you much. What difference does it make, anyway?"

"Probably none. It was just one of the places Ro-Jo suggested that I might look for Harry. I thought that if you had a key, I could get in without any trouble."

"Go by the realtors' office. Tell them you're in the market."

I put the Big Red on the coffee table and spread my hands to indicate my sweatshirt and torn jeans.

"I'm sure they'd believe I'm a high roller."

"OK, maybe not. Are you gonna look for Harry in there?"

"Maybe. But I want you to find out who owns the place. With your connections it should be easy."

"All right, I can do that, I guess. But what are you going to do?"

"First of all, I'm going to try having a talk with Ro-Jo. I want to know just exactly what he told the other man looking for Harry."

"You should've thought about that yesterday."

"I did, but I didn't see the need to question him more closely. I didn't know I was going to be shot at."

"You keep bringing that up. You don't sound too happy about it."

"Would you be?"

"Probably not, but you don't know for sure that it has anything to do with Harry. What would anybody want with him?"

"That's what I'd like to know."

"Are you gonna keep looking?"

I said that I was, but there was something in my voice that must have bothered Dino.

"It's not going to be like the last time," he said.

"You don't know that. It's not starting off very well."

"Look, Harry's just an old guy who goes around Dumpster diving and living off the streets. Nobody's after him for anything. What happened last night was just an accident."

"No," I said. "It wasn't an accident. One shot can be an

accident, but not five or six. Somebody was trying to put me out of commission."

"OK, say that's true. All the more reason you need to find Harry."

I didn't say anything.

"You'll find him," Dino told me. "You'll find him before the other guy does."

I picked up my glass and swallowed the last of the Big Red. "I wish I could be as sure of that as you are," I said.

▽

8

RO-JO WASN'T ANYWHERE around the 61st Street Pier. I drove down 61st, which in spite of its palm-lined esplanade is a lot like a midway filled with a little of everything: tire stores, gas-and-go food stores, pet shops, guitar stores, fast-food restaurants, and bait shops. Most of the bait shops are close to Offats Bayou, which by the time you get close to the causeway comes right up to the street and then goes under it. Sometimes I fish there when I don't want to go out on the pier.

I stopped at Jody's Bait and Tackle. According to the hand-painted signs on its flaking blue plywood walls, if you didn't want squid or mullet or bait shrimp, you could buy table shrimp instead.

When I fished, I usually bought my bait shrimp from Jody, and he knew Ro-Jo and Harry, both of whom occasionally scavenged along the street.

Jody's place was lighted inside by a couple of bare fluorescent bulbs, and the smell of shrimp and fish was nearly overpowering. There were some dusty rods and plastic lures on the wall, and some reels in a glass case. Jody, a heavyset black man, was behind the beat-up counter.

"What's biting today?" I asked him.

"Same thing that was bitin' yesterday," he answered. "Nothin'." He looked me over. "Speakin' of bitin', somethin' bite your face?"

"My cat," I said.

"You got to watch them cats. They bad about that."

"You selling any bait?"

"With the fish not bitin'? You old enough to know better than that."

"Maybe things will pick up."

He shrugged. "Business always slow this time of year. I never thought I was gonna get rich sellin' fish bait. You want some shrimp?"

"Not today. I'm looking for somebody."

"Who might that be?"

"Outside Harry," I said. "Or Ro-Jo. Either one."

He thought for a second. "Now that you mention him, I ain't seen Harry in quite a spell. What you think he up to?"

"I wish I knew. Dino's worried about him."

Jody knew Dino. Everyone who had lived most of his life on the Island knew Dino, even if he didn't like to get out of the house.

"Harry and Dino, now there's a pair. They pals?"

"That's what Dino tells me."

"Huh. I guess it could happen, but they a funny set of buddies if you ask me. Ro-Jo Dino's pal too?"

"Not that I know of. I want to ask Ro-Jo something about Harry."

"Ro-Jo by here yesterday, but I ain't seen him since."

"What time yesterday?"

Jody looked at an old green and white Dr Pepper clock on the wall above my head. The black numbers were faded, but you could still see them.

"Just about this time. Say he goin' up to the Randall's."

Randall's was the big supermarket in the shopping center not far up the street. I didn't think Ro-Jo would be going in the front door. I thanked Jody for the information and started to leave.

"You sure you don't want some bait? Little mullet, maybe? You never can tell when them fish gonna start in to bitin'."

"Not today. I'll be back tomorrow."

"That what you say now. Don't do my pocketbook no good."

I turned back and put my last ten on the counter. "Do you have a piece of paper and a pencil?"

He reached under the counter and brought out a stained notepad and the stub of a pencil that had the paint chewed off. I wrote my number and Dino's on it.

"If you see Ro-Jo, tell him I want to talk to him," I said. "Then call me. If you can't get me at home, call Dino. That's his number." I put my finger on it.

He covered the bill with his big hand. "I be sure to do that," he said.

I went on up to Randall's, hoping that Ro-Jo might be sticking to a kind of schedule. Harry was like that. He went by certain places at the same time every day, and Randall's was close to a cafeteria where Ro-Jo might go looking for a bite to eat if the grocery store didn't work out.

Ro-Jo wasn't at the fragrant Dumpster behind Randall's, however, nor was he behind the cafeteria. With the money I'd given him the day before, he could have afforded to go through the line, but that wasn't his style.

It was mine, however, so I went in. Feeling in need of some serious cholesterol and fat, I had a bacon and cheese steak, some macaroni and cheese, and some fried okra. I topped it off with two whole wheat rolls. I didn't get any butter for the rolls. Just call me a health-food freak.

When I'd eaten, I paid with one of the fifties Dino had given me and got change. Then I decided to go back to Dino's. He could easily have found out by now who owned The Island Retreat, even if it was a Sunday. He'd resent my interrupting the play-off game, but that was his tough luck. He should be thankful that I'd decided not to beat him up.

Dino wasn't watching the game. He was talking on his portable telephone when he came to the door, and the TV set wasn't even on.

"Son of a bitch," he said as he opened the door for me. He didn't say it to me. He was talking to whoever was on the phone. "Are they sure it's him?"

He listened for a few seconds. I couldn't make out what the voice on the other end of the line was saying, but I could tell that Dino didn't like it. His knuckles were white, and if the phone hadn't been made of sturdy plastic he might have crushed it.

"God damn," he said. And then he said it again. "God damn." He listened some more. "All right. All right. Thanks for calling. Yeah. Right. I'll keep it quiet."

He looked right at me when he said the last part, and I knew he wasn't going to keep anything quiet. He was going to tell me as soon as he hung up the phone, or turned it off, or whatever it is that you do to portable phones.

This one you turned off, which is what he did after saying "Yeah" and "Right" a few more times. Then he set the phone on the coffee table and looked at me.

"You want some Big Red?"

"Not now. What was that all about?"

Dino sat on the couch. So did I.

"You remember Braddy Macklin?" he asked.

Nobody who ever met Braddy was likely to forget him. He was about five-ten and as close as you can come to a hundred and eighty pounds of solid muscle. He could make a fist that looked like it could punch through a concrete wall, and it probably could. Of course that was more than thirty years ago, when I was just a kid.

"I remember Braddy," I said. "What about him?"

"Somebody killed him."

"You mean he died?"

Braddy Macklin would have to be somewhere in his seventies by now. He'd been the bodyguard for the uncles in the wide-open days, and the toughest-looking man I'd ever seen.

"I mean somebody killed him. That was a guy I know on the cops. They found his body about an hour ago."

"I didn't even know he was still around. Did you ever see him?"

Dino looked a little sorry, whether for himself or Macklin I didn't know.

"No. I never see anybody much. You know that. I talked to him on the phone once in a while. Not often."

"And somebody killed him."

I still couldn't believe it. Who'd kill a man that age? Leave him alone and he'll be dead soon enough.

"Yeah." Dino looked at the floor and shook his head. He couldn't believe it either. "Somebody killed him. And that's not all."

"What else?"

"They found him in The Island Retreat."

"What the hell was he doing there?"

Dino folded his arms and leaned back on the couch. "That's what the cops would like to know."

▽

9

DINO HAD BEEN busy. While I was talking to Jody and eating a high-fat special, he'd been calling a few people he knew. The interesting thing was that he hadn't been able to find out who owned The Island Retreat.

"Some corporation," he said. "That's all the realtor knows. And he wasn't happy that I called him during the pre-game."

"OK. We can worry about that later. What about Braddy Macklin?"

"The cops got one of those anonymous calls this morning. Some guy tells them there's a dead man in The Island Retreat. They go down there to check it out and find Braddy. Jesus, Tru, that old guy used to ride us around on his shoulders when we were kids."

Dino didn't usually get sentimental, and I didn't want to encourage him.

"I remember," I said. "What else did the cops find?"

"Not a damn thing, at least not as far as my guy could tell me. Braddy was shot a couple of times, but I don't know what with or how long he'd been there."

I'd been shot at recently too, and I wondered if there was a connection between what had happened to me and what had happened to Braddy. As I said, I don't believe in coincidence. One old man missing, and another old man murdered. That probably wasn't a coincidence either, and if one of the two had been shot, what did that mean for the other? Finding Harry was beginning to seem more urgent by the moment.

"Braddy has a kid," Dino said, interrupting my thoughts.

"A kid? At his age?"

"I don't mean a *kid* kid. She's nearly as old as we are."

I wondered how old he meant. When I was thirty, I thought anyone else would have to be at least twenty-nine to be nearly as old as I was. Now that I was long past thirty, I figured that people even ten years younger were nearly my age.

"Does she live on the Island?" I asked.

"Yeah. She manages a motel out on the seawall."

I thought that I might want to talk to her later. Right now, finding Harry seemed more important.

"About The Retreat," Dino said. "There's something else you need to know."

"So tell me."

"The realtor told me he's had a lot of calls on it the last couple of weeks. Gambling's a hot topic again, and there's a rumor that Galveston's going to vote it in. So The Retreat would be a natural. It's got a history, and some of the old furnishings are still there. Not the roulette wheel or the slots, maybe, but the dining tables, the kitchen, stuff like that."

Dino was right about the history. The Texas Rangers had dumped all the slots into Galveston Bay, and the roulette wheel was probably there too.

"Someone's always trying to get gambling voted back into Galveston," I said. "Just about every year, in fact. It never wins."

"This time it might," Dino said. "We've already got the cruise ship that takes people out past the three-mile limit, and there's that dog track just a few miles up the interstate in La Marque. The state has a lottery, and those Indians out in El Paso or wherever they are keep pushing for casino gambling on their reservation. And there'll be horse racing in Houston later this year. People around here don't want all the gambling money going over to other places. Much less Louisiana."

Lake Charles already had riverboat gambling, and I'd heard that interests in Houston were looking into something similar. Maybe gambling did have a chance at a comeback in Galveston after all.

"Did your realtor friend say who was interested in The Retreat?" I asked.

"Heavy hitters, he said. That could mean anything. One group has a couple of big-name baseball players in it. Retired players, he said."

"Let's get back to the heavy hitters. He probably didn't mean that they had a three hundred average. You have any thoughts on that?"

"You can probably guess."

I could, of course. As long as the uncles were in power, Galveston had never worried about organized crime getting involved in the gambling. The uncles didn't count. They were local boys, and local boys weren't considered organized crime because they had no connections to the mob. The uncles were criminals, or at least they were involved in highly illegal activities, but they were hometown boys and that made everything all right.

The respectable locals, the rich families who traced their ancestry back to the previous century and their fortunes back to shipping, banking, and insurance, were comfortable with the uncles. They brought in big-name Hollywood entertainers, they kept the town's secrets, and they avoided messy situations that would bring bad publicity to themselves or the community.

There were scandals, of course. The gambling and prostitution were an open secret all over the state. But most Texans regard themselves as independent thinkers who don't mind a little illegality as long as it's under control. They were willing to leave Galveston alone to go its own way, or most of them were.

It was a fine situation for the old families, who regarded

themselves as the real rulers of the city. The uncles were keeping the Island alive. Houston had taken over most of the shipping, and while the banking and insurance money was still in town, it wasn't flashy and it didn't provide many jobs. Gambling did, though of course the patriarchs avoided any involvement in it. It wouldn't have been seemly. In fact, it would have been downright disastrous for their standing in the community.

So everyone was happy with the way things were, except of course for a few preachers and do-gooders and others opposed to gambling on moral grounds, and the big boys in the East, who weren't getting a cut of the action. But the uncles had the muscle to keep out any and all competition.

The uncles couldn't keep the Texas Rangers out forever, though, and when the state eventually got an attorney general who listened to the do-gooders and took his office seriously enough to include cleaning up the Island in his duties, the uncles reluctantly went out of business.

Now it appeared that gambling might make a return, and if it did, there would be huge sums of money involved, money that would attract a lot of types the uncles had kept well away from Galveston during their watch. Unfortunately, the uncles had been gone for a long time.

"First Harry and now Braddy," Dino said. "What's going on here, Tru?"

"I don't know. I was hoping you could tell me, but you say you don't know any more than I do."

"It's the truth, damn it. I was just worried about Harry. I didn't know anybody was going to get killed, much less Braddy Macklin. What are you going to do about it?"

"You told me this was going to be easy," I said, feeling a little sorry for myself.

Dino didn't sympathize. "OK, so I lied. But I didn't know I was lying when I asked you to look for Harry. Are you gonna help me out here or not?"

I wanted to say no. I wanted to go home and read my book and listen to old songs on the CD player.

Instead I said, "I'll keep looking for Harry."

"Great. Maybe you oughta talk to Cathy Macklin, too."

"Braddy's daughter?"

"Yeah. If there's some connection between Harry's going missing and Braddy's getting shot, maybe she knows something."

Maybe she did, but I didn't think this was the time to talk to her.

"You can pay a sympathy call," Dino said.

"She's probably at the funeral home, making arrangements. I don't want to bother her now. Anyway, you seem to know her. Why don't you go see her?"

Dino looked around the room at his TV set, his VCR, his new Super Nintendo system. He didn't look at the curtained windows or the door.

"I don't get out much," he said.

"You found me on the pier yesterday," I pointed out.

"Yeah, and I went out to the house and fed your cat."

"Quite a day, all right," I said. "You should try it more often. I bet Evelyn would like to see you more than she does. Maybe even eat at Gaido's or some place like that."

Dino squirmed on the couch. He wasn't like me. He didn't eat out, not even without Ray there to fix his meals for him. He ate a lot of TV dinners and canned chili.

"I don't think she'd like that," he said finally. "People would talk about us."

"Nobody knows where she used to work," I said.

"Somebody might. Nobody ever forgets anything on this Island."

"Why don't you ask her if it would bother her to be seen in public with you?"

Dino stood up. "How'd we get on this subject?"

"We were talking about you going to see the Macklin woman. What was her name?"

"Cathy. I don't want to go."

"It would be the right thing to do. Braddy Macklin was a friend of yours. He worked for your uncles."

He sucked in a breath and let it out very slowly. "All right, I'll go. But you gotta go with me."

I decided to humor him. "All right."

"But not until after the game," he said, reaching down for a remote.

He punched a button and the TV set came to life. The Cowboys were lined up on somebody's forty-yard line, and a little digital clock in the lower right corner was ticking off the seconds left in the half.

"I'm going to look for Ro-Jo some more," I said. "I left your number with someone who might see him. If he calls, get the information."

Dino was watching the TV intently. It was almost as if he'd forgotten I was there.

"Yeah," he said. "I'll do that."

"I'll be back in a couple of hours," I said.

"Right. I'll be ready."

I wondered if he really would.

▽

10

THERE WAS A stiff breeze blowing in off the Gulf, and I could smell the strong seaweed odor of the beach. The clouds were still thick and gray. I drove the Jeep through the Sunday traffic along Broadway. Most of the tourists would be going to The Strand, headed for the Island's restored nineteenth-century buildings filled with dress shops, antique stores, and restaurants. Or maybe they'd go to Pier 21 and watch the slide show about the Great Storm of 1900.

I kept an eye out for Ro-Jo. He wasn't anywhere in sight. I drove along the seawall and checked out the alleys behind the motels, but he wasn't there either, and he wasn't behind any of the supermarkets or the smaller mom and pop grocery stores.

There were a few people on the beach, but most of them looked cold and miserable. The waves were whitecapping and slamming into the marble jetties. The only happy creatures were a dog chasing an inflated ball bobbing in the rough surf, a kid throwing corn chips in the air to some screaming gulls, and the gulls who were getting fed.

I wondered about the cats. It wasn't high tide yet, but there hadn't been any sign of them at the 61st Street Pier.

There was no sign of Ro-Jo, either. He had disappeared just as effectively as Harry had, and I wondered if it might have been for the same reason. There were plenty of places either of them could be, but I was sure now that The Island Retreat wasn't one of them. I'd give a lot to know why Ro-Jo had mentioned it to me, but I'd have to find him before I could get the answer to that one.

I drove out toward the house where I was living. It was surprising how soon after leaving the seawall I was surrounded by reminders of the Island's past. Where once there had been ranches there were now small pastures, but cattle still grazed there. Every now and then you could even see a corral full of horses and someone riding.

I thought that Ro-Jo might have found someone to take him in. He might even have straight friends with whom he could live for weeks. I didn't know. He was just someone I saw and talked to occasionally.

Locating people who live an average existence is a lot easier that finding someone like Ro-Jo. Most of us leave traces. We use credit cards or the telephone. We have employers and pay taxes. We use the services of the state, the city, and the county. We engage in all sorts of transactions that are recorded in one place or another.

But not people like Ro-Jo. He might have gone to school at one time or another, but I couldn't find him through academic records because I didn't know what his real first name was, and as far as I knew he didn't even *have* a last name. If he'd ever paid taxes, which I doubted, it had been a long time ago. He didn't use the homeless shelters, and he didn't have credit cards. He didn't use the phone. Who would he call? In some ways it was as if he didn't even exist. Harry was the same way, only worse, because he was even farther removed from the system than Ro-Jo.

When it was time to go back to Dino's, I was no farther along than I had been when I'd left, but it occurred to me that there was something else I could do.

I could go to the police.

I knew that Dino would blow up if I suggested that idea to him. He had his contacts on the force, but he didn't deal with the cops officially. He used me for that.

Not so long ago, Evelyn had gotten mixed up in a murder by being at the wrong place at the wrong time, and Dino had asked me to look into it. I'd talked to a cop named Gerald

Barnes, who knew me from the case involving Dino's daughter. Barnes wasn't especially fond of me, but I'd helped him out a little, so he'd probably talk to me if he was on duty.

Dino wouldn't mind waiting a little longer. In fact, he'd probably be glad for the delay.

The Galveston Police Department is located behind the city hall in a square, unattractive building with a lot of glass and a few scrawny oaks in front. All the lower limbs have been trimmed off the oaks, maybe so that no one can climb them and peek into the second floor, which is solid with windows. The building is on 26th and Avenue H. Or Ball Street. Quite a few Galveston streets have more than one name.

There's a stop sign on Avenue H that has another sign under it, white with black letters:

LOOK BOTH WAYS

I'd never been sure whether the sign was there to remind the cops or the average driver, though it didn't say much for the mentality of either. Maybe it was there because the fire station was right on the other side of the police department and the city was trying to reduce its liability if someone got flattened by a fire truck.

I would have parked in the lot by the police department, but all the places are reserved for the people who work there. Of course, most of the spots were vacant because it was Sunday, but I wouldn't have been surprised if the cops had come out and ticketed the Jeep had I been so bold as to park it where it didn't belong. I parked on the street.

The inside of the building smelled of cigarette smoke. Two cops were in the hall smoking and looked at me but didn't say anything. Barnes was at his desk fiddling with some papers when I walked in. There weren't a lot of papers to fiddle with, since Barnes kept his desk a lot neater than most cops. The top was nearly bare. There wasn't even an ashtray, and there were no cigarette burns along the edges. Unlike most cops, Barnes didn't smoke, and apparently he didn't allow the alleged lawbreakers to smoke at his desk. There was a half-full coffee cup, a couple of chewed yellow pencils, a few papers. That was it.

He glanced up when he saw me standing there. He didn't look much like a cop. His brown hair was getting thin on top, and his brown eyes were mild behind his glasses. He might have been an insurance salesman or a teacher for all the clues his appearance gave.

His eyes hardened when he saw me, however. "I should've known," he said.

I sat in the straight-backed chair beside his desk. "Known what?"

"That you'd show up. If I'd thought about it, I would have known."

He picked up one of the pencils from the desktop and rolled it around between the fingers of his right hand.

"I can tell you're glad to see me," I said.

"I'm not glad to see you. I don't want you messing around in this."

I tried to pretend ignorance. "Messing around in what?"

He pointed the pencil at me. "Don't give me that crap. You know what I mean. One of Dino's old buddies gets whacked, and the next thing I know, here you are. I should've known."

"Which one of Dino's old buddies are we talking about? I didn't even know Dino had any buddies except me."

"He had Ray," Barnes said.

I didn't want to talk about that. I said, "I didn't expect to find you here on a Sunday."

He laid the pencil back on the desk. "Don't give me that crap, Smith. You knew I'd be working on the Macklin case or you wouldn't be here."

"Macklin?"

"Oh, for God's sake. You know who I'm talking about. I'm just surprised you didn't show up sooner."

I didn't string him along any longer. He wasn't having as much fun as I was.

"All right," I said. "I know about Macklin. But Dino didn't send me. He doesn't even know I'm here."

"Yeah, I'll bet he doesn't."

"Look, Barnes, I know you don't like me much, but I solved that case for you back on Mother's Day. Maybe I can help you with this one."

"You didn't solve that case," he said. "I did."

"OK, you solved it. But I don't think you could have done it without my help."

He picked up the pencil and doodled on the back of one of the pieces of paper for a second or two. Then he put the pencil down and looked at me.

"All right. So you made a suggestion that helped me crack that one. That doesn't mean I like civilians fooling around with murder cases."

"I'm not fooling around in a murder case. I'm working on something entirely different. I just wondered if the two were connected."

I went on to tell him about Harry. When I came to the part about getting shot at, he nearly jumped out of his chair.

"Damn it, Smith, you should've come to us last night!"

I admitted that he might have a point. "But I don't see what you could have done," I added.

"We could get the slugs, run some tests. See if they're from the same gun that shot Macklin."

I reminded him that I didn't know about Macklin when I was dodging bullets. And then I mentioned that the slugs were on government property.

"How many forms would you have to fill out before they let you get close to that old building?" I asked.

He leaned back in his chair. "Too damn many."

"But I might be able to get them," I said. "Unofficially."

He wasn't comfortable with that idea. "We couldn't use them as evidence."

"You wouldn't need them for that. But it might be nice to know if they came from the same gun."

"I'm not saying you should get them," he told me. "I don't encourage trespassing. But if you just happened to have one, and if you left it with me, I might get it tested."

That was all that needed saying on that topic. Now that I'd softened him up, I asked about Macklin.

"How'd he get into The Island Retreat? I thought that place was locked up tight."

"That's a good question," Barnes said. "The place *is* locked up tight, and the windows are boarded up. If you find out how he got in, let me know."

"There's not a hole in the floor? That you can climb up to on the pilings?"

Barnes looked at me as if I might be crazy. "Now you're yanking my chain. You think a guy in his seventies or older climbed up the pilings and through a hole in the floor? I'm not sure *I* could climb those pilings, and I'm in a lot better shape than some guy that age."

"So there's not a hole in the floor?"

"Hell, no. There's no hole in the floor or the roof or the walls. Where'd you get an idea like that?"

Another black mark for Ro-Jo. "I just thought there had to be a way in, and that might be it. Maybe the person who shot Macklin had a key."

"Very clever, Sherlock. Now tell me how he got it."

I couldn't do that, so I changed the subject by asking how long Macklin had been dead.

"I can't tell you that until after the autopsy."

"You've been involved with homicides before, though. You could guess."

"I don't like guessing."

"I don't blame you. Call it an estimate."

He still didn't like the idea, but he said, "He'd been there for a while. A week or more. He wasn't fresh."

"How was he killed?"

That was the kind of question Barnes was comfortable with. "Shot twice in the chest with a nine-millimeter pistol. I'd guess a Glock, but we'll know for sure after the ballistics tests come back. He was armed, had a gun in his hand, but it hadn't been fired."

"What was he doing in The Island Retreat?"

"I thought that since we're working together now, you might tell me the answer to that one."

"I wouldn't be asking if I knew."

"Right. You're telling me that a guy who was as tight as Macklin was with the uncles winds up dead in The Retreat and Dino doesn't know a thing about it. My ass."

I didn't think a discussion of his anatomy would serve any useful purpose.

"It's the truth," I said. "He's as much in the dark on this as I am."

"Right. He's just trying to find his old friend Harry."

"That's what he told me."

"Then he's yanking *your* chain."

I didn't want to admit that the same thing had occurred to me. And that I hadn't entirely discounted it. So I didn't.

"I think he's telling the truth," I said. "I was there when he got the news about Macklin. He was as surprised as I was." I paused. "Have you talked to Macklin's daughter?"

"What do you think we are?" Barnes said. "Clowns? Of course we've talked to the daughter."

"And?"

"And she didn't have any idea why her old man was in The Retreat. I get the idea that they weren't the best of pals. But why am I telling you this?"

"Because you want my cooperation. You scratch my back, I scratch yours."

Barnes pulled off his glasses and rubbed the bridge of his nose. Then he settled the glasses back in place and sighed.

"I've been lied to by experts, Smith. You aren't an expert."

"You're going to hurt my feelings if you don't watch out," I said.

"Sure I am."

"OK, so you're not. But I do want to cooperate. If I find out who shot Macklin, you'll be the first to know."

"But you're just looking for good old Outside Harry," Barnes said.

"True. But you never know what I might run across while I'm doing it."

"And in return for your cooperation, or telling me what you run across, I'm going to keep you posted on whatever I find out about Macklin's murder."

"Don't call me," I said. "I'll call you."

"I'm sure you will, but I don't know how much good it's going to do you."

"We'll just have to wait and see, then, won't we?"

He smiled, but it wasn't a pleasant smile. "Yeah. We'll just have to wait and see."

"One other thing," I said, not quite willing to give up on Ro-Jo. "Were there any signs that anyone else had been in The Retreat?"

"You're kidding me, right? There's a dead man on the floor, he's been shot twice, and you want to know if anyone else had been there. Who do you think shot Macklin? He damn sure didn't do it himself."

"I meant did you see any old cans, old newspapers lying around, that kind of thing?"

"There wasn't anything like that. We'd have found it. Why?"

"I was just wondering," I said.

"Already holding out, aren't you?" Barnes said. "I knew it."

"I'm not holding out. I was just wondering about something."

"And you're not going to tell me what it is, are you?"

He was right. I wasn't.

He said, "Get out of here, Smith," and I started for the door.

"Another thing," he said, and I turned back.

"What?"

"Don't call me."

I smiled and waved good-bye. I would have blown him a kiss, but he might have taken it the wrong way.

▽

11

I DIDN'T SEE any need to mention to Dino that I'd talked to Barnes. He wouldn't like it, and I hadn't learned anything useful. Maybe later I'd bring it up. If I had to.

Dino didn't say anything about my being late when I got to his house. He was too excited about the football game.

"Dallas is in the finals again," he told me. "That Emmitt Smith is the best damn runner I've seen since you. Too bad you never got a shot at the pros."

"We all know whose fault that is," I said.

I tried to keep it light, but Dino's face fell.

"Ah, hell, Tru," he said.

"Think nothing of it. I probably never would've made it through training camp."

He started to disagree, then changed his mind. "You find Ro-Jo?"

"Not a sign of him. Did Jody call?"

"Nope. No calls."

"You ready to go see Macklin's daughter?"

"Hell no. But I said I'd go, and I will. You think we should call first?"

"What, and lose the element of surprise?"

"You want to surprise her?"

"Not especially. But if the great recluse Dino shows up at her door, she's going to be surprised. You can count on it."

"I don't know why you have to joke about everything. I'm gonna call her."

"Good idea," I said.

* * *

Cathy Macklin, as it turned out, wasn't the manager of the Seawall Courts. She was the sole owner and proprietor.

"My father bought the place for me," she said, brushing her dark hair out of her face. "To make up for never having a thing to do with me for the first twenty years or so of my life."

She looked at Dino when she said it, as if he were somehow responsible, but it was the uncles who were to blame if anyone was. Guarding their bodies was bound to take up a lot of a man's time.

We were in the manager's unit of the motel, which was designed to look as if it had been built in the 1950s and hadn't aged since then. It was out past the old Fort Crockett area, down in a sort of depression behind the seawall, and the individual units were square stucco modules on stilts. You couldn't see the stilts from the street, just the tops of the units. We had to enter from a side street that dipped down below the seawall.

"The stilts are for when it rains," Cathy Macklin had told us. "This place can flood in ten minutes if it's raining hard enough. I've had people leave in a panic, but there's nothing to be afraid of. The water never gets more than a few inches deep."

Ms. Macklin was about thirty-five, I thought, though I could have been off by a few years either way. I'm not a good judge of people's ages. She had black hair with only a strand or two of gray in it, a wide mouth, clear skin, and amazingly blue eyes.

I particularly liked the eyes. It was her attitude that bothered me.

"I don't know what you two want," she went on after explaining how she got the motel in response to our opening conversational gambit. "But then I don't much *care* what you want. I'm really not interested in the sympathy of my father's former associates."

"We weren't exactly his associates," I said.

"Whatever you were. I'm not interested in digging up the past."

I tried to remember whether I'd ever seen her when I was a kid. If I had, she hadn't made an impression. I had better taste now.

"We're sorry about Braddy," Dino said. "He was a friend of mine a long time ago, and I liked him. But that's not really why we're here."

Dino looked even more uncomfortable than I felt. He was out of his own environment, and to make matters worse he'd had to ride in the Jeep. As much as I didn't like the job he'd stuck me with, the look on his face when I told him to get in was worth a lot. He'd zipped his blue and white Dallas Cowboy jacket all the way to his chin and put on a pair of sunglasses to give himself that anonymous look. And now he was being forced to sit in a strange room and talk to someone he didn't know. I thought he was doing pretty well so far, however.

"Why are you here, then?" Cathy Macklin asked.

"We think your father's death might be connected to something I'm working on," I told her. "The disappearance of a friend of ours."

She gave me a thoughtful look. I didn't mind. It gave me a chance to stare at those eyes some more.

"What happened to your face?" she asked.

"I ran into a door."

"Oh," she said. "Well, let me tell you something."

I was willing to let her tell me just about anything. I liked her voice, which was a little husky, as if she'd been a smoker at some time in the past.

"My father and I didn't see much of one another," she said. "He wasn't really into what they call 'parenting' these days. Even when the gambling closed down, he spent most of his time looking out for a couple of criminals. He didn't have time for me and my mother. As far as we were concerned, he was just someone who came around on birthdays and holidays, and most of the time not even then."

I said, "And you don't care who killed him?"

"He was my father, so I care at least a little, but it's not my job to find out. That's something for the police to worry about. I've got a motel to run."

"Everyone has a job to do," I said. "Mine is to find an old man who's gone missing."

"I don't see what that has to do with me or my father."

"Maybe nothing," I told her. "We'd just like to check it out. If you'll just answer a few questions for us, we won't bother you again."

I didn't add that I'd like to bother her again, but not about her father's murder. I wanted to find out a few more things about her, such as whether she might like to go out with me and whether her eyes were really that blue or if she was wearing colored contact lenses.

"All right," she said. "Ask your questions. And then leave me alone."

I asked her the things I wanted to know: what her father was doing in The Island Retreat, who he'd been talking to lately, what they had discussed, and whether he knew Outside Harry.

She couldn't help me with anything. She knew who Harry was because she'd seen him on the streets, but she had no idea who her father had associated with or what he'd been up to lately.

"I told you," she said. "My father and I didn't see much of one another. We didn't talk on the phone, we didn't visit. Maybe if he'd needed me for something, I would have gone to him. But he was in good health, he had plenty of money, and he didn't need anyone for anything. Or if he did, it wasn't me that he needed. So I'm afraid I don't have any information that would help you."

"If you think of something, I hope you'll let us know," Dino said. "We really need to find Harry. We're afraid he might wind up dead, like your dad."

"I hope not," she said, as if she might actually care. "But I don't know any more than I've told you."

We thanked her for her time, extended our unwanted sympathy again, and left.

"What do you think?" Dino asked me as we pulled out of the parking space under the manager's unit.

"I believe her," I said.

"Damn," he said. "So do I."

He was obviously uncomfortable with the wind blowing his hair and pulling at his jacket, but he didn't complain as we drove back to his house. I had to give him credit for that. Still, the look on his face when I stopped at his curb was like one you might see on a drowning man's who's just discovered that he can breathe underwater. It was all he could do to keep from bolting for his front door without even saying good-bye.

"You're gonna keep on looking, right?" he said.

I told him that I was, and he was out of the Jeep and headed down the sidewalk.

"Wait a minute," I said.

He turned around, but he kept edging along the walk toward the door.

"Why don't you give Evelyn a call, ask her if she'd like to go eat with us? We could try one of those fancy restaurants on The Strand."

"Maybe later," he said. "You should be out there looking for Harry. Tonight might be the time to find him."

I could tell that he didn't really believe it, but that was all right. Neither did I.

▽

12

I DIDN'T LOOK too hard that night. It was even colder than the night before, and if Harry and Ro-Jo were around they'd be somewhere warmer than the street. There was no need to try The Island Retreat because obviously Ro-Jo had lied to me about Harry's hideouts, just as he'd lied to someone else. There were plenty of other places Harry could be, but I couldn't look in every vacant building in Galveston.

So after a few passes along the back alleys, I went home and read *Look Homeward, Angel* and listened to my CDs while Nameless slept on my bed. I was at a dead end unless someone came up with something to help me out, and I couldn't figure out who that someone might be.

I couldn't just forget about Harry, however. I was worried about him and what might happen to him. This was all Dino's fault, and even after pulling out my billfold and counting the money Dino had forced on me, I wasn't happy about having taken on the job. If Harry got killed, I was going to feel guilty for a long time, and tomorrow I had to go in and work for Wally Zintner's bail bond service. I didn't think Wally would be sympathetic if I asked for time off to do a job for someone else. And Eugene Gant thought *he* had problems. I would've traded places with him in a New York minute.

That night I dreamed I was running in a race. It was an unusual race, since it seemed to have no beginning and no end. I ran all night long, and when I woke up I was as tired as if the race had been real.

* * *

The little building where I worked was only a couple of blocks from the police department. Although the owner's name is Wally Zintner, the place is called AAA Bail Bonds on the theory that most people generally call the first place they see in the Yellow Pages. A bonding agency named Zintner's wouldn't stand a chance.

The outside of the building doesn't look like much. The sign is faded, and one of the windows has a long crack that's been patched up with duct tape. The tape's been there for so long that it's tearing along the crack in a place or two.

The inside isn't any better. The walls are cheap paneling, there's no pad under the carpet, which is frayed and stained where people have spilled soft drinks on it, and all the desks have ashtrays that look as if they haven't been emptied in weeks. The smell of smoke is stronger than in the police department. The furnishings consist of four desks and a Coke machine.

There were clerks at three of the four desks. The fourth one was shared by me and Dale Becker, Zintner's bounty hunter. We also shared the office computer, though as far as I knew Becker never used it.

The clerks—Betsy Carver, Ronnie Slane, Nancy Lamb—were all smoking. There was already a thin gray cloud gathering near the ceiling. Only Nancy had a client; the others were on the phones. The client, who was also smoking, didn't look happy, but then that wasn't unusual. Hardly any of our clients ever looked happy. Neither would you if you were in the clutches of Wally Zintner.

I waved to Nancy and went back into Zintner's office, which was really nothing more than a small area set off from the rest of the big main room by a couple of beaverboard partitions. It didn't even have a ceiling. There was room inside for Zintner, his chair, a very small desk, and a visitor's chair. There was also room for me if I slid along the beaverboard.

"Hey, Smith," Zintner said when I entered. I didn't have

to knock. There wasn't a door. "What happened to your face?"

I was already getting tired of that question. "I cut myself when I was shaving," I said.

"I hate it when that happens. What's going on with you lately?"

He already knew, of course. He always knew what was going on almost as soon as Dino did. Sometimes he knew sooner.

"Why don't you tell me?" I said.

He grinned. He was one of the skinniest men I knew, probably wore a size twenty-four belt. He always wore tight blue jeans, a pressed white shirt, high-heeled boots, and a black bolo tie with a turquoise pull. Not to mention a belt with a silver buckle in the shape of the state of Texas. He was always complaining about business, but I knew he'd made a pile of money.

"Sit down," he said. "Let's talk over old times."

I preferred to stand. Sitting in the visitor's chair made me feel cramped and trapped. A roach ran out from a hole in the carpet and crossed under the desk. I didn't bother to try to step on it. I figured that it would develop bronchitis and die if it hung around long enough.

"What old times?" I asked.

"You know. The old times when Dino's uncles had a free hand and there was a slot machine in every cathouse in town."

"I didn't know you went back that far."

"Hell, I'm BOI, Smith. You know that. I wasn't in business then, but I was old enough to know what was going on."

"Do you know what's going on now?"

"I know Braddy Macklin's dead, if that's what you mean."

"Do you know why?" It was worth a shot. He might even tell me.

"If I did, I'd be over at the cop shop spilling the beans," he said. "You know us bondsmen. Always at the service of law and order."

There were a lot of people who would argue with that. They want to get rid of bail bonding companies because they see the chance that county courts can be victimized. A week or so back, there was a mild outcry in Houston when someone found out that a couple of bonding companies were posting bonds against the estimated value of property rather than the assessed value. Zintner would never do anything like that, or at least I didn't think he would, but he wasn't exactly what I thought of as the police force's best friend.

I did think, however, that I might as well play along with him. "I'm glad to hear you're so eager to help out the forces of good. It makes it easier for me to ask a little favor of you."

"Uh-oh," he said. "Here it comes."

"Here *what* comes?" Dale Becker asked, looming in the doorway to the cubicle.

Becker looked like a pro wrestler—huge and beefy with long blond hair, a gold loop in his right earlobe, and a mean mouth that twisted in a perpetual sneer. He wore an L. A. Raiders cap that he'd turned backwards so that the bill covered his red neck, and his jeans were so tight you could count the money in his wallet. Becker didn't like me, which made us even. I didn't like him, either.

"Smith here was just about to ask me a favor," Zintner said.

Unlike me, Zintner thinks Becker is the greatest thing since tail fins on cars, and even I have to admit that Becker is good at what he does. He always gets his man, and usually without too much of a struggle. Of course, the fact that he looks as if he could break your back with one hand tied behind him makes things easier.

"He wants you to let me help him find old Outside Harry," Becker said. "I bet that's what it is."

"So you're looking for Harry?" Zintner said. He didn't sound surprised. "What the hell for?"

"Yeah," Becker said. "What the hell for?"

"I don't remember inviting you in here," I said.

Becker laughed. It came out something like, "Hunh-

hunh-hunh." Beavis and Butt-head without the charm.

"You might as well tell us, Tru," Zintner said. "It'll be all over the Island by noon."

It seemed as if it were all over the Island already, so I told them. I didn't mention that Macklin's death might be connected; after all, it might not.

"I didn't know Dino was into helping out old bums who scrounge in trash cans," Becker said.

"Dino likes to help his friends," I told him.

Becker snorted. "Some friend."

Zintner went on as if Becker hadn't spoken. "And you want some time off to help out. Is that it?"

"You guessed it."

"What about me?" Becker said. "I bet I can find him in fifteen minutes."

"I'm sure you could," I said, not meaning a word of it.

Oh, Becker could find people if he got a tip, and he had plenty of people who were eager to feed him information, but no one was going to tip him to Harry. He could also bring people in if someone else located them by phone, and lately that someone else was always me.

"I don't know that I can give you any time off, Smith," Zintner said. "Tomorrow's Tuesday. Check-in day. We'll need you on the phones."

On check-in day, the clients, well over a hundred of them, would be calling in to report their whereabouts. All of them would call, because Zintner had a hand on their pocketbooks. Something like that got their attention in a way that a probation officer never could.

"What about Dale?" I asked. "He could take a few calls."

Becker laughed again. "I don't do calls," he said. "I nab the bail jumpers."

"You might as well give it a shot," Zintner told Dale. "Why not? It wouldn't hurt you to do a little phone work. Nobody's jumped, as far as I know. But if I need you here, Smith, you better get your ass back whether you've found Harry or not."

"No problem," I said.

"You think there's any connection between Harry and what happened to Macklin?" he asked.

"Macklin?" Becker said. "Braddy Macklin? Didn't somebody ice him last night?"

That's the way Becker talks. He thinks it makes him sound tough. Maybe it does.

"Yeah, somebody whacked him," Zintner said. "You know, Harry's been around a long time. He was as old as Macklin, maybe older. Two old guys like that, one of 'em dead and another one missing, there might be some connection."

"Who cares?" Becker asked. "Two dudes that old, they got no business taking up space."

I wondered if he'd feel that way if he happened to live as long as Harry and Macklin had. He was a sensitive guy, Becker was, and it was no wonder I didn't like him. But at least he hadn't asked about my face. I had to give him credit for that.

"Tell you what, Smith," Zintner said. "You can take all the time you need. I didn't know Harry, but I've been seeing him on the streets since I was a kid. And if you need any help, give Becker a call. He might as well be out and doing something as sitting on his ass here. After tomorrow that is. I gotta have somebody on the phones tomorrow."

Becker started to protest at the mention of the phones, but then he changed his mind. He just grunted, turned in the doorway, which wasn't easy considering his size, and walked back into the main room.

"Listen, Smith," Zintner said, "you don't want to go getting mixed up in anything that might get you killed. Braddy Macklin was a tough old bird."

"I'm not going to get killed," I said. "I'm just looking for Harry."

"Sure. You got a gun?"

"Not with me," I said.

He opened the bottom drawer of his desk and pulled out a Glock 17.

"You sure you're not carrying?

"No," I said. "It's against the law."

"Better safe than sorry."

He sounded like something out of *Poor Richard's Almanack*. He must have been really worried about me. Maybe he knew something I didn't know. But when I asked him, he denied it.

"I just don't believe in taking chances," he said, putting the Glock back in the drawer and closing it.

"Me neither," I told him. And I meant it.

▽

13

I WAS ON my way out of the building when Nancy Lamb called me over to her desk. Her client was gone, and she was holding the phone.

"Telephone for you, Tru," she said, and handed it to me.

"Truman Smith," I said into the mouthpiece.

"Good morning, Mr. Smith." The voice was a little shaky, and had a wheeze in it. An old man's voice. "This is Patrick Lytle."

"Good morning, Mr. Lytle." I tried to keep the surprise out of my voice. Lytle was a member of one of the oldest families on the Island. I couldn't imagine what he could possibly want with me, unless some member of his family needed bail money. "What can I do for you?"

"I understand that you're looking for Harry Mercer," he said.

"Harry Mercer?"

"You might know him better as 'Outside' Harry."

"Oh," I said, always quick with a comeback. Until that moment, I hadn't even known that Harry had a last name. "That's right."

"I'd like to talk to you about Harry if it's convenient," Lytle said. "Like you, I'm quite interested in his whereabouts."

Harry was getting more popular by the minute, which was a little surprising, but I wasn't going to question my good luck. Maybe Lytle had some information I could use. I didn't have anywhere else to look.

"I'd be glad to talk to you," I said. "When and where?"

"I don't get out much these days," Lytle wheezed. "Would it be convenient for you to come by my home this morning?"

"Any time," I said.

"Fine. Let's make it eleven o'clock. Do you know where the house is?"

I told him that I knew.

"Very well. I'll see that the gate is open."

When I hung up, Nancy was looking up at me. "Was that *the* Patrick Lytle?" she asked.

"The one and only."

"And you're going to his house?"

"At eleven o'clock," I said.

"I'd give a lot to see the inside of that place. You need any company?"

I wouldn't have minded having Nancy along, but for some reason I didn't think Lytle would approve.

"You think Zintner would give you the time off?" I asked.

She sighed and lit a cigarette. "Probably not. But I've wondered about that house since I was a kid."

"So have I," I said. "I'll tell you all about it."

She exhaled a stream of smoke that rose to join the rest of the pollutants collecting near the ceiling.

"You'd better," she said, "or I'll make you really sorry."

"He's pretty damn sorry already," Dale Becker said from the desk where he was sitting.

"What's the matter with him?" Nancy asked me.

"Jealous of my good looks," I said, and left before he could get out of his chair and ruin them with his baseball bat.

Lytle's house was in one of the older parts of the city, where some of the houses looked as if they would be right at home if they were moved to San Francisco. They were narrow, several stories tall, and so close together that the neighbors could have reached out their windows and shaken hands.

Lytle's house, however, wasn't like that at all. It wasn't

even what I'd call a house. It was a mansion, and along with its grounds it occupied about half an entire block.

If you were just driving by, you might think that no one lived there. The grounds were enclosed by a rusty wrought-iron fence about five feet high, and the house was hard to see from the street because it was surrounded by huge palms that grew closely together, and by giant magnolias and oaks that hadn't been trimmed in forty years or more. The oaks were the oldest of the trees, and Spanish moss hung from them like long gray beards. They must have been older than the house itself, and that dated from somewhere just after the turn of the century. The magnolias weren't much younger.

The house hadn't been kept up any better than the trees. The porch columns were nearly bare of paint, and what few flakes remained on the house were faded almost colorless. I had been a housepainter only recently, but I couldn't even begin to estimate how many gallons of paint would be required to cover the Lytle mansion again, or how many hours it would take to get the job done. I was just very glad that I wasn't going to have to paint it.

As Lytle had promised, the gate was open. I drove through, the branches of an oak brushing my head as I passed under it. Either Lytle didn't get many visitors, or those he had didn't mind having their cars scraped by oak limbs.

I got out of the Jeep and walked to the porch. It was a little like walking through the jungle. The grass hadn't been trimmed back from the sidewalk in quite a while, and only about half its width was visible.

The porch roof rose up two stories above my head, and I wondered how many people it would take to encircle the columns with their arms. Three? Four?

There was no doorbell, but there was a large brass knocker covered with greenish corrosion. I used it to give a few discreet taps.

I didn't hear any footsteps in the hallway, but the door swung open. There was a young man standing there, about twenty-five, maybe a year or two older. He was good-looking in an outdoorsy sort of way, and he was wearing rubber-soled hiking boots, which is why I hadn't heard him in the hall.

"Truman Smith?" he asked. He didn't look especially happy to see me.

"That's me," I said. I would have given him a card, but I don't have any cards.

"Come on in," he said, and I did.

I gave my surroundings a once-over so I could report to Nancy, who was going to be disappointed if she thought the house was filled with magnificent treasures. The hallway was completely bare, from its tile floor to its high ceiling. The wallpaper was peeling away, and in places it was completely missing. I could see something that looked like canvas on the walls.

"He's back in his room," the young man said, and turned down the hall. "You can follow me."

I tagged along obediently, and we entered what must have been the living room at one time. Or maybe it would have been called the parlor. It was nearly as bare as the hallway, and the little furniture it contained was covered with dusty cloths that swept down to the floor. The chandelier was nice, however.

We went through that room and down another hall, where the young man stopped and knocked on a door. Without waiting for an answer, he swung the door open.

"Here's Mr. Smith," he said, motioning for me to enter.

I walked past him and into a room right out of the nineteenth century. It held a canopy bed, an armoire with mirrored doors, a writing desk, a washstand with a basin and pitcher sitting on it, and a spindly-legged wooden chair with an embroidered cushion.

There were only two modern things in the room. One was a thirteen-inch TV set on a small table. The other was a La-Z-Boy recliner in which a white-haired man was sitting with a blanket over his legs. There was a smell of mustiness and medication in the air, as if the window hadn't been opened in years, which it probably hadn't.

"Thank you, Paul," the man said. It was the same voice I'd heard on the phone. "You may leave us now."

There was no reply, but I heard the door close behind me.

"I am Patrick Lytle," the white-haired man said.

I guessed his age at about eighty. His arms were thin and his eyes were watery, but he had the clear skin of a man of thirty. I wondered what his secret was.

"You'll excuse me if I remain seated." He gestured to the blanket. "I no longer have the use of my legs."

"I'm sorry," I said.

"Don't be. It happened a long time ago, and I'm quite used to it now. It's really no great loss. I find that staying at home is preferable in many ways to leaving it. Paul keeps me well supplied with whatever small needs I might have."

"Paul is your son?" There seemed to be a family resemblance.

"My grandson. I have no surviving children, Mr. Smith. But I'm forgetting my manners. Please have a seat."

I wasn't sure the spindly chair would hold me, but it did. I didn't bother trying to get comfortable. In that chair, comfort would have been impossible.

"Are you a private investigator, Mr. Smith?" Lytle asked.

"I have a license. I don't practice often."

"I've seen private investigators on television," he said. "Magnum. Cannon. Names like that."

"Smith sounds kind of dull in that company," I said. "Maybe I should change it to something ballistic."

"The name isn't important. The man is. I remember you from your glory days." He was no doubt talking about football, though I didn't know whether he meant my high school career or the abbreviated one I'd had in college. "Have you changed since then?"

In more ways than you'd ever understand, I thought. What I said was, "Some."

"I'm sure you have. You must be more prudent now, less inclined to take chances."

I didn't know what he was getting at, but I thought I might as well listen. Maybe eventually he'd tell me.

"There was a time," he said, "when the Island meant something to people, when the people who lived here were willing to take risks to make it better. Have you looked at it lately, Mr. Smith? Really looked at it?"

"Yes," I said. "Have you?"

He shook his head. "I know quite enough without having to see it. The deserted downtown, half the buildings boarded up, the fried-chicken franchises, the houses that are practically falling down. Galveston's time has passed, Mr. Smith."

That wasn't the whole truth, and I had a feeling that he knew it. There was a lot going on in Galveston, what with the restoration of so many of the old buildings in the area of The Strand, the Mardi Gras celebration every year, the condos that seemed to be popping up like mushrooms, Moody Gardens, the steadily improving tourist trade.

I mentioned a few of those things.

"They amount to very little," he said. "What the Island needs is a massive injection of capital, not these piddling stopgap measures. It needs men of vision, men of purpose."

I started to ask him if he was one of those men, but I thought better of it. Anyone taking a look at his house, which seemed to represent the very decay he was worried about, would know he wasn't the kind of man he thought the town needed.

"Some are going to say that the answer to our problems is gambling," he went on. "Gambling is an evil, Mr. Smith. It must not be permitted to return to the Island."

A lot of people felt that way, and probably a lot of them were members of families like Lytle's, families that went back to the days when Galveston was the jewel of the Gulf Coast. But I couldn't figure out what any of this had to do with Outside Harry.

I would have asked Lytle, but he was already going along his own path, and I didn't want to interrupt.

"Someone killed Braddy Macklin last night," he said, looking at his TV set. "It was on the news."

I'm sure it was, but I seldom watch the news on television. It always begins with the latest car wreck, murder, or child abuse case, and the more blood they can show, the better. Stories like that are generally buried on the second or third page of one of the inside sections of a newspaper, which is one reason I prefer getting my news from them.

"Macklin," Lytle said, "was a scourge on this city. He was scum. He was a reminder of all that was bad about Galveston."

"Gambling brought a lot of people here," I said. "It gave a lot of people work. I don't remember much about crime in those days, but it seems to me we have a lot more now."

I don't know why I was defending gambling. Maybe because Dino was my friend and his uncles had run the gambling. Or maybe it was because of Cathy Macklin's blue eyes. Neither was much of a reason, I have to admit.

Lytle waved a hand as if brushing away a bothersome fly. "Gambling is itself a crime. They try to soften it these days, call it 'gaming,' but that doesn't change it. We can't allow its return."

I didn't ask who he meant by *we*. The conversation was getting stranger and stranger.

"I'm not sure what this has to do with Harry Mercer," I said.

Lytle twitched a little, as if I'd surprised him by my rudeness in changing the subject.

"Harry Mercer," he said, "is this Island's past. He is the opposite of criminals like Braddy Macklin. Whoever shot Macklin did the city a favor, let me assure you."

Maybe he was right about Macklin. Even his daughter didn't seem to have liked him very much. But I didn't see his point about Harry.

"Harry isn't exactly a pillar of the community," I said.

"Perhaps not. But he is self-sufficient. He goes back to a time when the Island was more than just a place for tourists and sightseers. He is an important part of our history. He is widely known and liked. He is a friend to everyone, children and adults alike. I want you to find him and bring him to me. I want to help him establish a permanent place to live."

I thought that Lytle was guilty of romanticizing the past, just as I'd done when I spoke out in favor of gambling. Harry was an old man who ate dog food sandwiches. A nice enough guy, sure, but not the key to Galveston's future. Still, if Lytle wanted to offer him a home, I wasn't going to stand in the way. That is, I wasn't if I could even find Harry and if he wanted a home after I found him.

"I can't promise to bring him to you," I said. "He might not want to come. All I want to do is find him and be sure that he's all right."

"I have a servants' quarters," Lytle said. "Just behind the house. Not that I intend for Harry to become my servant. Far from it. He'll be provided with whatever he needs, and I'll never disturb him."

I wondered if he had even heard a word I'd said.

"I can't bring Harry here if he doesn't want to come," I told him, speaking a little louder than necessary.

"He'll come, I'm sure of that. Just tell him what I have to offer. That's all I ask."

I could promise that without any trouble. I did, and then I stood up to go.

"I hope you can find him, Mr. Smith," Lytle said. "My grandson will see you out."

Almost as he finished speaking the door swung open and Paul Lytle was standing there.

"One moment," his grandfather said. "I forgot to ask you, Mr. Smith. What are your rates?"

"I already have a client," I said. "It wouldn't be ethical for me to take your money too."

"And who is your client?"

I started to tell him, but then I changed my mind. It wasn't any of his business. And he might not have liked the answer.

"That's privileged information," I said.

For a second his old eyes lit up, and I thought he might challenge me. But then he sank back in his chair and his chin dropped to his chest.

"I'll see you to the door now," Paul Lytle said, and I followed him out of the room.

When I drove away from the mansion, I turned the corner and looked to my left. The side of the house was almost obscured by the trees, but I thought I could see the window of the room where Lytle was sitting.

And I thought I could see someone watching me, but I didn't know who or why.

▽

14

PATRICK LYTLE, I thought, was a lot like Dino. If he ever left his house, he would probably panic. I wondered if he watched Oprah and Geraldo and all the rest.

He was also trapped by a past that he didn't really understand, not if he thought that Outside Harry was a glorious representative of it. In short, Lytle was probably a little crazy, not that there was anything wrong with that. Some of my best friends were a little crazy. For that matter, I was probably a little crazy too.

And for some reason that train of thought made me think of Sally West. I stopped at a store for a bottle of Mogen David wine and drove to her house, which was right on Broadway and even older than Lytle's mansion.

The old black man named John answered the door. He never changed from year to year. Sally was ninety now, and while he probably wasn't quite that old, he was at least as old as Patrick Lytle.

"Hello, Mr. Truman," he said. He always said that. "Miss Sally's in the parlor."

He took the wine. "Thank you, John," I said, and followed him to the parlor, where he announced me and then melted away.

Sally West was small and frail. She wasn't in mourning, but she was dressed in black, as she had been every time I'd seen her. She was sitting in a cane-bottomed rocker and, like Lytle, she didn't get up when I entered the room. She could if she had to, but it took more effort then she wanted to expend. Despite her age, her eyes were bright and sharp and her voice was crisp.

"Hello, Truman," she said. "You do have some news for me, I hope."

"A little," I said.

"Oh, good. Then sit down and tell it to me."

I sat in a rocker just like the one she was using and told her about Braddy Macklin's murder, Outside Harry's disappearance, and my visit to Patrick Lytle. While I was talking, John came back in with some of the wine in crystal glasses on a silver tray. The wine bottle was on the tray as well, and he set it on a small table by Sally's chair. Then he handed us the glasses and vanished again.

When I had finished the story, Sally had finished her first glass of wine, so I got up and poured her another. I had hardly tasted mine. I wasn't as fond of Mogen David as Sally was.

"You have wonderful stories, Truman," she said. "And you do lead the most exciting life of anyone I know. Hearing you makes me wish you could come by more often. Is there anything I can tell you in return?"

Dino had introduced me to Sally when I'd first come back to the Island. She was a wonderful source of information about the old days, and she loved to gossip, or to "exchange information," as she put it. To her, it wasn't gossiping. Not to me, either. It was just talking to a friend. Sally had a lot of friends, and she knew almost as much about the Island's present as about its past.

"You could tell me something about Patrick Lytle," I said.

If anyone would know about Lytle, Sally would. On the wall beyond where she sat there was a dark mark painted to indicate the level to which the flood waters had risen in 1900. There was a lot of other history in the room as well. Sally's family had been on the Island as long as nearly any other, and her house and mind were repositories of the Island's lore.

"I'm sure you already know a great deal about Mr. Lytle," she said.

"Just stories I've heard. Nothing I'd put much stock in."

"Most of the stories are probably true. He's lived in that house since he was a boy, just as I've lived in this one. Neither of us gets out much anymore." She took a sip of wine. "He must be a bit like me, living in the past more than the present."

For Sally the past began long before the days when Dino's uncles were running the show on the Island. She didn't resent the gambling days the way Lytle seemed to, and in fact she seemed to have enjoyed them, but she thought that the early decades of the century were the time when Galveston was really alive. From my conversation with Lytle, I suspected that he felt much the same way.

Sally interrupted my thoughts. "How is our friend Dino these days?"

"He's still not getting out much," I said.

"I'm not at all surprised. But didn't you tell me that he was getting better about that?"

"He is," I said. "But not as much as he should be."

Sally had a theory about Dino. She believed that he was a victim of some sort of paralysis of will. Trapped by the legend of his uncles and unable to do anything to bring back the kind of glory they represented to the Island, he shut himself away from the responsibility he believed he had. And from the possibility of failure.

"You've been good for him, though," Sally said. "You've helped take his mind off himself."

"It hasn't been me so much," I said. "It's just that things have been happening. They haven't been such good things, either."

They hadn't, but they'd been as good for me as for Dino. I'd been so depressed about Jan that I'd just about dropped out of life until Dino got me involved in finding his daughter.

"You shouldn't judge things so hastily," Sally told me. "Wait a few years. Time gives you a much better perspective."

I wondered if I would have her perspective even if I lived as long as she had. I doubted it.

"What was Lytle's attitude toward the uncles?" I asked, getting back to the subject I'd come about. "And about gambling in general?"

"There's a story there," Sally said. "Would you refill my glass, please, Tru?"

I did, and then she told me the story. It was one I hadn't heard before, but that was because I was too young to know about it when it happened.

"Braddy Macklin stole Patrick Lytle's wife," she said. "Her name was Laurel, and she was a lovely girl. She dearly loved to gamble. That's how she met Braddy, you see. His own wife didn't approve of gambling, and she didn't approve of Braddy's job. He came off the docks, and his wife thought of that as good, clean work. It was hard, of course, but decent. She never forgave him for going to work for Dino's uncles, and their relationship was quite strained."

She looked at me over the top of her wineglass. "You know that a certain kind of woman is attracted to a rugged man, one who looks as if he might have the potential for violence?"

I hoped she didn't think I was like that. "I can imagine it," I said.

"Laurel Lytle was like that, and it showed. Braddy wasn't immune to that kind of silent flattery, and before long they were an item."

That went a long way toward explaining Lytle's feelings about Macklin and about gambling on the Island. Or that's what I thought until Sally went on with her story.

"Patrick Lytle didn't seem to mind," she said. "I don't recall that he was much of a gambler, though he may have been. Either way, he did nothing to prevent his wife from going to The Island Retreat. I'm sure that if you could see any of the newspapers from that time, you'd find her in the background of some of the photographs they took when the stars came to town."

"What happened to her?" I asked.

Sally smiled. "That's the mysterious part of the story. She

disappeared." I was about to interrupt, but Sally stopped me. "Don't get excited. It's not as interesting as I'm trying to make it sound. Braddy Macklin didn't kill her, and Patrick Lytle didn't bury her in the backyard. It was all much more mundane. She apparently told several of her friends that she was getting bored with life on the Island and that she was going to ask Patrick for a divorce. She said she was thinking of going to Las Vegas. Maybe to California. After the divorce, she simply packed up and left."

"So what's the mystery?"

"Only that no one ever heard from her again. Some of us expected that she might turn up in a movie, perhaps in a bit part. Or, failing that, perhaps become the mistress of some notorious gangster. I suppose that the truth was much more tiresome. She probably married some colorless individual exactly like Patrick and lived miserably ever after."

I wondered if that was true. And I wondered if Laurel Lytle was back in town. Stranger things had happened.

"There's a grandson," I said. "Paul. He was at the house today."

"Oh, yes. Paul. He was the son of Laurel's daughter, Mary Elizabeth. Mary Beth, she was called. She grew up here on the Island, but she left as soon as she graduated from high school. Did you know her?"

I vaguely recalled a girl a few years older than I was. In those days, a few years made a lot of difference, especially if it was the girl who was older.

"I think I remember her," I said. "But I didn't know her."

"There was some kind of problem between her and her father, but whatever it was, they kept it in the family."

I took that to mean that Sally hadn't been able to find out what the problem was.

"At any rate," Sally went on, "she went to school out of state, married, and had a son. Soon after that, both she and her husband were killed in a traffic accident. They were on the way home from a party, and he tried to beat a train to a crossing. He didn't, and they both died instantly. The son was sent here to live with his grandfather, and I think he's been quite a help."

"What about the old man's legs?" I asked.

"I'm not sure I like hearing you call him an 'old man,' " Sally said. "He's not nearly as old as I am."

"I didn't mean that he was old," I apologized. "I just meant that he's older than his grandson."

"That's all right, then. Patrick was in an accident, too, but his involved something other than a car and a train. He told everyone that he fell."

There was something about the way she spoke the last sentence that sparked my curiosity.

"Don't you believe him?"

"I'm not sure. There was always something unconvincing in his story."

"What?"

For a second she rocked in her chair. Then she said, "He was always such a careful man that it was hard for me to believe that he could fall in his own house. I suppose that the insurance company believed him. He was rumored to have gotten a fair settlement from them."

There wasn't much evidence of any money from insurance or anywhere else in Lytle's house now, but I wasn't really worried about Lytle's legs, so I moved on to other things.

"What had Braddy Macklin been up to lately?" I asked.

"I don't really know much about him. But I do know that he was interested in buying The Island Retreat."

"What? Did he have the money? Did—"

"Don't get excited. I don't know much about it. And I don't think he was interested for himself. He was undoubtedly representing someone else."

"Are you sure? Even Dino doesn't know about that."

She smiled, a trifle smugly. "Dino doesn't know *everything*."

"All right. Who else is involved?"

"I haven't found that out yet. I'm sure you will, however, and then you'll tell me."

I promised that I would give it a good try. "What about Macklin's enemies?"

"Most of them are dead. But if he was thinking of helping bring gambling back to the Island, you can be sure that he had enemies. Some of them from the old days, some of them from now. That's something else for you to find out."

I wondered if Macklin's daughter would know. Even if she didn't, I wouldn't mind talking to her again.

"Lytle isn't exactly living in the lap of luxury," I said. "What happened to his money?"

"That's another mystery," Sally said. "His family was in textiles, I believe, and they made a sizeable fortune before the cotton market collapsed. Somehow he didn't manage to keep much of it, only enough to hold onto the house."

Holding onto it was all he was doing. There was furniture in the bedroom, but I suspected that most of the rest of the place was as bare as the parlor had been. The furniture that Nancy thought was there had probably been sold to antique dealers many years before.

"I'm afraid I haven't helped you very much," Sally said.

"You've given me a lot to think about, and a lot to work on. I have one more thing to ask, if you don't mind."

"I don't mind. I'm glad for the company."

As usual, I promised myself that I'd get by to see her more often. I always meant it at the time.

"Do you know anything about Harry Mercer?"

"Only what you know. I used to see him prowling the streets when I was younger and got out of the house. He's been on the Island a long time."

She wasn't able to tell me any more, and when I left her I had more questions than answers. But I thought they were questions that would get me closer to Harry. If they weren't, they were questions that would get me closer to whoever killed Braddy Macklin, and though I wasn't sure I cared about that, I felt more than ever that Macklin and Harry were somehow connected.

By the time I got to the Jeep, I thought I knew how.

▽

15

THE WEATHER HADN'T improved since the day before, and by the time I got to Dino's house it was raining. It's bad enough in the Jeep when it's cold; rain is *really* miserable. Luckily, I got to Dino's before I got soaked.

Dino was watching Phil Donahue, and he made me wait until a commercial came on before he'd talk to me. I don't think he was really that interested in Münchhausen by Proxy Syndrome, but he said he was. He did, however, turn off the set when I started talking. I filled him in on my visit with Lytle and told him what I'd learned from Sally.

"Are you sure you didn't know about Macklin representing someone wanting to buy The Retreat?" I asked.

Dino shook his head. "Sure I'm sure. I tell you what, Tru, if I didn't know better, I'd think you didn't trust me."

"I trust you. More or less."

"More or less. Maybe we could go on TV. Friends who don't trust friends." He clapped me on the shoulder. "Hey, it's nearly noon. You want some lunch? I got a couple of roast beef dinners, or maybe you'd like some Mexican food. How about enchilada dinners?"

"We'll go out," I said.

"What are you talking about? It's raining. We'll get drenched. I can pop a couple of those babies in the oven, they'll be ready in a jiffy."

"Get your raincoat," I said.

* * *

We went to Shrimp and Stuff, which was close and cheap

and probably the only place in town where you could still get a shrimp dinner for just over five dollars. Of course you have to order it at the counter, wait for your number to be called, and eat off a styrofoam plate, but that doesn't affect the taste of the food.

"I'll probably get pneumonia," Dino said while we were waiting for our food.

"No you won't. It was hardly raining, and you were wrapped up in that coat."

"Yeah. As if that helped."

He looked really uncomfortable, and he kept glancing around the room to see if anyone was staring at him.

"Stop whining," I told him. "Did you know about Macklin and Mrs. Lytle?"

"I probably heard about it. I don't remember. I was just a kid at the time."

"What about Macklin's enemies. Anybody want to kill him that you remember?"

"What's all this harping on Macklin? You're supposed to be looking for Harry."

"I am."

"You must be pretty sure the two of them are connected, then."

I looked around the room. Shrimp and Stuff was a little more yuppified than it had once been. There were even a few baskets of ivy, which looked imitation to me, suspended from the ceiling. The clientele was still the same, though, mostly locals with a couple of tourists thrown in. Nobody seemed interested in our conversation.

"Maybe Harry knows who killed Macklin," I said.

That got Dino's interest. "How?"

"Maybe he saw the murder."

While it was true that Barnes had told me there was no hole in the floor of The Island Retreat, it had occurred to me that he might be wrong. The police wouldn't have been looking for it, and it could have been concealed somehow. Maybe it wasn't even in the same room where Macklin had been shot. The fact that there was no trash around didn't mean anything either. Harry might have been more careful in The Retreat than he'd been at the lab, if he was the one who'd left the trash at the lab. I was just guessing that he was; it could have been anyone. Even Ro-Jo.

"So someone's after Harry because he can put the finger on him," Dino said.

"It's a possibility."

"You think Harry's already dead?"

That was another possibility, one that I didn't want to think about. I'd been worried enough when there had seemed to be only a vague connection between Harry and Macklin. And while this new connection was anything but solid, I was even more worried now.

"Well," Dino said, "what do you think?"

I was saved from answering when the woman behind the counter called our number. Dino and I got up to get our trays. We both asked for extra helpings of the red sauce, which was the best in town. For a few minutes we were too busy eating to talk, but Dino finished off a hush puppy and asked me again.

"What do you think about Harry? You think somebody's killed him like they killed Macklin?"

The truth was that I didn't have any idea. "I hope not," I said. Then I added, "If he's dead, he hasn't turned up anywhere."

"So what're you gonna do?"

"I'm going home and read a book," I said, dipping a fried shrimp in red sauce.

Dino stared at me.

"Look," I said, "I don't have any idea where Harry could be. I don't even know who to ask. If Ro-Jo shows up, I can ask him, but now he's lost too. So what I'm going to do is wait until after dark. Then I'm going to check out The Retreat if I can get inside. Harry might be there, for all we know."

I didn't mention going by the old marine lab to look for

the bullets, since Dino didn't know I'd discussed that with Barnes. But I intended to do that, too.

Dino looked skeptical. "Harry wouldn't be in The Retreat, not after the cops have been there."

"Why not? It's the safest place in Galveston right now."

I thought it was a good point, but Dino didn't agree. He had other ideas about what I should be doing.

"You oughta go talk to Cathy Macklin," he said. "See if she can tell you anything else about her old man. Like who he was enemies with in the old days. There must still be some of those guys around."

"You'd be the one who'd know about that," I said.

"Is that a crack? You still don't trust me?"

"I didn't mean it that way. I just thought you might know. Or be able to find out."

He ate his last french fry. When he was finished chewing, he said, "I might. I could do it on the phone."

"Good. I'll take you home."

"And then what? Go read your book?"

"We'll see," I said.

Dino wasn't happy with that answer, but at least it had stopped raining and we didn't get wet on the way back to his house.

I probably would have read the book, but there was someone at the house when I got there. He was sitting in a big black Mercedes sedan, looking out through the windshield at the bay. You couldn't see the Gulf from the house.

Nameless wasn't much of a guard cat. He was sitting on the porch, waiting for someone to open the door and let him in. The guy in the car wasn't bothering him at all. If the guy had some Tender Vittles, Nameless would probably go off with him.

When I stopped the Jeep, the visitor got out of the Mercedes. He was tall, taller than I am, and much wider through the shoulders. He was wearing an expensively tailored suit, not exactly the preferred Island wear even in the winter, but his face didn't match his outfit. It was a hard face, one that you could strike a match on, and the eyes were like black marbles.

He walked over to the Jeep. "Your name Smith?"

"That's right," I told him. And then to prove that I had a snappy comeback for every occasion, I asked, "What's yours?"

For a second I thought he wasn't going to tell me. He just stood there and looked at me out of those hard black eyes, as if he wasn't sure whether to break my neck then or wait until a little later. The way he was built, he could do it whenever he wanted.

But he didn't break anything. He told me his name.

"Alexander Minor," he said. "You can call me Alex. I want to ask you something."

I got out of the Jeep and walked past him to the house. I opened the door and let Nameless in. Then I turned to Minor.

"You want to come inside?" I asked.

He didn't. He wanted to get whatever it was that he'd come for and get out of there. But he didn't say that. He just walked over to where I was holding the door open and went in the house.

My parlor wasn't as bare as Patrick Lytle's, but it didn't look like anything in this month's *House Beautiful* either. There was an old couch covered with something that might once have served as the seatcovers on a twenty-year-old Plymouth and a couple of chairs. Aside from an old Quasar TV set on a cabinet, that was it.

"Have a seat," I said.

Minor looked at the couch with distaste.

"It's clean," I said. "The cat hasn't started shedding yet this year."

Minor sat down. I left him there and went into the kitchen. Nameless was standing patiently by his bowl, and I put about half a pack of Tender Vittles in it. He started purring and eating at the same time. I don't know how he does that.

Minor was still on the couch when I went back into the living room. I'd sort of hoped he'd be gone, though of course I'd known he wouldn't.

"They tell me you find people," he said.

I sat in one of the chairs. "Who's 'they'?"

"Cop named Barnes."

It figured. If you're a guy like Minor, you want to let the cops know you're in town. They're going to find out soon enough, and if you've already talked to them, you're covered.

"He's wrong," I said. "I *used* to find people. That was a long time ago."

"That's not what Barnes says. He says you're looking for some guy right now."

"Barnes has a big mouth."

Minor nodded. "Cops are like that." The voice of experience.

"Who did he tell you I was looking for?" I asked.

"Guy named Harry."

There was no use denying it. "All right. I'm doing a favor for a friend. What does that have to do with anything?"

Minor put his right ankle up on his left knee. His shoes were handmade and worth more than Dino had paid me so far. I thought about asking for a raise.

"I'm looking for the same guy," he said.

Somehow I wasn't surprised. "Why?"

"I'm an attorney," Minor said.

Now I was surprised. "An attorney?"

"Right. Like I went to law school, passed the bar. You got a problem with that?"

The problem was that he didn't look like an attorney. He looked like somebody's hired muscle, if not something worse. Naturally I didn't want to tell him that. He might take the opportunity to prove that I was right. He certainly looked as if he'd enjoy it.

"No problem," I said. "I was just wondering why you were looking for Harry. What's his last name, by the way?"

"What, you don't know it?"

"Not until today," I said. "And he's been around here all my life."

"It's Mercer, Harry Mercer. And don't ask me his middle initial. I don't know it."

"Why are you looking for him?"

Minor didn't hesitate. "He has some money coming to him."

I held in a laugh. "Money? Harry?"

"He had a sister," Minor said. "In Dallas." He pulled an envelope out of his suit coat and handed it to me. "It's all in there."

I took the envelope and removed the letter. The sister, Gennie Mercer, said she was employing the firm of Minor and Douglass to look for her brother in the matter of an inheritance. It could have been written by anyone; it could even have been genuine.

"I didn't know Harry had a sister," I said.

That didn't bother Minor. "You didn't know his last name until today."

He had me there. "What do you want from me?"

"I want you to help me find Harry Mercer," he said.

▽

16

WHEN MINOR HAD gone, I went into the bedroom, put on the five-CD set of Elvis's fifties recordings, set the player to shuffle, and listened for a while. Nameless came in, but he didn't listen long. He went to sleep.

Minor was lying about why he wanted Harry, and he was no more an attorney than I could sing like Elvis. Barnes would have known that too, and he'd probably sicced Minor on me just to stir the pot and see what rose to the top.

I figured that Minor was tied in with one or the other of the gambling interests, maybe even the same people Macklin had been hooked up with. If that was the case, then he was in town to find out who'd killed Macklin.

If that weren't the case, Minor might even be the killer. He certainly looked the part.

But how did he know about Harry? The answer had to be Barnes again. I'd underestimated Barnes. He'd figured out from my questions that I thought Harry was in The Retreat when Macklin was killed.

Minor would have gone to the cops first, found out all they knew, and then started using it. He would have had plenty of time to fix up the phony letter. The right people, and he would know them, could have told him all about Harry. Even that he had a last name.

Minor's attorney cover didn't have to stand up to close inspection. All he had to do was stay out of trouble long enough to find Harry. Then Harry would tell him who killed

Macklin. Or Minor would kill Harry to eliminate the only witness. I didn't know what Minor's job would be after that.

I'd told Minor the same thing I'd told Lytle, that I already had a client and that I couldn't help him. He tried to make it "worth my while," as he put it, but I didn't let him.

He took my refusal better than I'd thought he might, but I knew that didn't mean a thing. I'd have to watch my back from here on out. If Minor couldn't find Harry on his own, he'd be lurking around. Of course, I'd been intending to keep a close watch on my back. After all, I'd already been shot at.

Which reminded me. I got out of the chair and walked to the little closet in the side wall of the room. I had to reach high up on the shelf to get the box I wanted. I took it over to the bed and opened it. The sheepskin-lined leather case was still there. I took out the case and undid the zipper. The 7.65 mm Mauser—you can call it a Luger if you want to—was inside. I returned the box to the closet.

There was another box I had to get, but it was in a drawer in the kitchen. I follow gun safety precautions. I keep the pistol and the cartridges in separate rooms.

Of course, if anyone were to break in the house with evil intentions, I'd be dead before I could find the pistol, run to another room for the cartridges, and load the clip. On the other hand, I would never shoot myself with a pistol that was supposed to be unloaded.

I took the cartridges into the bedroom and got the pistol. Nameless watched me with gray-green eyes, not any more interested in what I was doing than he was interested in the voice of Elvis Presley, who was now singing "I Was the One."

I took the pistol and cartridges into the living room. The TV set was on a cabinet with sliding wooden doors. My pistol-cleaning gear was in the cabinet. I got it out and enjoyed the oily smell of the rags for a minute before I cleaned the Mauser. Then I loaded the clip.

OK, so it was against the law to carry a pistol. I was going to take the chance; it would be a lot more effective against a threat on my life than carrying something equally illegal like, say, half a dozen dildos. If someone took another shot at me, I was going to shoot back, though I didn't intend to kill anyone, not if I could avoid it. I just didn't like working at a disadvantage.

I put the pistol back in the case and zipped it up. I read a few more chapters in *Look Homeward, Angel,* and then it was time to go to work.

It wasn't really work, however. I was talking to Cathy Macklin again, so it was more pleasure than business. For me. She looked at things a little differently.

"I told you before, Mr. Smith. I don't really know anything about my father."

"Call me Truman," I said.

She smiled at that. It was a very nice smile, and it lit up her blue eyes.

"I didn't know anyone was named Truman anymore," she said.

"There aren't very many of us. But we're all men of sterling character. Also we're hungry all the time. Would you go to dinner with me?"

She didn't know how to take that. Maybe I was rushing things a little.

"It might be easier to talk over a meal," I said. "And you might even find out that you like me."

"Anything's possible," she said, though she didn't sound as if she really believed it.

"Is that a yes?"

"I have a motel to run," she said. Then, seeing my disappointment, she added, "But I suppose I could get Barbara to take over."

I asked her who Barbara was.

"She's a friend. She's also my assistant manager when I need a break. She comes in and answers the phone, takes reservations, handles registration for the drop-ins."

"Do you take a lot of breaks?"

"Very few, actually, but you look like you might be worth talking to."

"Some people think I tell interesting stories," I said. "Most of them are a lot older than you, though. The people, I mean, not the stories."

"I suppose it wouldn't hurt to take a chance," she said. "I don't take many of them, either, and Barbara tells me I should take a few more."

I liked Barbara already.

We went to Gaido's, which I liked because of the giant mutant crab perched over the door as much as the food, even though the food was quite likely the best on the Island. It was also considerably more expensive than my lunch had been, though that didn't matter. The company made up for it.

During dinner I found out a little more about Cathy Macklin, about how she felt growing up with an absentee father, about how easy and difficult at the same time it was to plan a funeral for him, about her college days at TCU, about the husband who'd left her after a brief marriage, about how much she liked living on the Island and being able to walk across the street anytime she felt like sticking a toe in the Gulf.

"A lot of BOIs don't like the Gulf," I said.

"That's their problem," she told me, cracking a crab claw. "I love it."

I told her a little about myself, too, about coming back to the Island to look for Jan, about finding Dino's daughter, about the murdered alligator. I didn't tell her much about looking for Harry, however. Finally, over a truly decadent dessert—vanilla ice cream rolled in pecans and topped with hot fudge—I got around to asking about her father's old enemies.

"There were probably a lot of them," she said. "But that was a long time ago."

"Can you remember anyone in particular? Anyone who might still be around?"

"I don't see what this has to do with finding your friend," she said.

I decided to trust her. You have to trust someone, and I didn't trust anyone else in this mess. So I told her my idea about Harry having witnessed the murder. I also told her about Alex Minor.

"So you have some competition," she said.

"That's right. And I don't want him to find Harry before I do."

"Why do you think he came to you? Was that smart?"

I'd been wondering about that myself, and while I had an answer, I wasn't sure it was the right one.

"It might not have been smart," I said, "but it was a calculated risk. He might have been able to buy me off. As it is, he knows that he wasn't given a false lead. I really am looking for Harry. Now he has a choice. He can keep on looking for Harry himself, or he can hang back and follow me, hoping I'll lead him where he wants to go."

"I wish I could help you," she said. "I really do. But I'm not sure I can."

"Just think. If you can come up with a name, that's more than I've got now."

"I'll try," she said.

The Jeep wasn't the most elegant mode of transportation on the Island, but Cathy Macklin liked it. She didn't even mind the way the wind messed up her hair. She asked me to take her for a drive down Broadway, and we passed some of the glories of Galveston's past: the old Gresham mansion, better known now as the Bishop's Palace; the refined lines of Ashton Villa; and the statue of Winged Victory that was dedicated to the memory of Texas heroes.

We also passed Sally West's house, and I casually mentioned that Sally was a friend of mine. Cathy was impressed.

"I'd like to meet her someday," she said.

"I'll introduce you," I promised, hoping that meant I'd see Cathy again.

We drove back down the other side of the esplanade, which was planted in tall palms and oleanders. The oleanders were green and thick, but there were no blooms this early in the year. Cathy's dark hair whipped in the wind.

"That was fun," she said when I took her back to the Seawall Courts. "I'm sorry I wasn't more help."

"That's all right," I said. "Maybe we could do it again."

"Maybe." She climbed out of the Jeep. "Barbara thinks you're cute. You could always ask her out if I'm busy."

I'd hardly spoken to Barbara when she arrived to take over the motel for Cathy. Barbara was about Cathy's age, and she seemed quite nice. But it wasn't Barbara I was interested in. There was something about Cathy that had attracted me from the first, and I wanted to see her again.

I got out to walk her up the stairs. "How do you know what Barbara thinks?"

"We have ways," she said. "You don't have to walk me up. I know the way."

I stood by the Jeep and watched her climb the stairs. About halfway up she stopped and turned.

"There was one man," she said. "I don't know if he's still alive."

"Who?" I asked.

"Lawrence Hobart. Have you ever heard of him?"

"Yes," I said. "I've heard of him."

I could have added to that, but I didn't. What I'd heard wasn't good.

▽

17

LIKE BRADDY MACKLIN, Lawrence Hobart, better known in certain circles as Larry the Hammer, had worked for the uncles, starting before Macklin had come along. Hobart's problem was that he couldn't resist the one thing he should have known better than to indulge in: gambling. Whenever he wasn't watching the uncles, he was playing the slots or shooting craps. Not in Galveston, however. He wasn't that dumb. He went up the road to Dickinson, where he thought he could get away with it.

The uncles found out, of course, and they ordered him to stop. Everywhere he went, he found that his credit was no good, and everyone was calling in his markers.

He got mad, he got drunk, and then he went after the uncles. Macklin was on the payroll by then, and he was the one who stopped the Hammer one night in The Retreat. The old-timers still talked about the fight, which became legendary. Within a few years, the entire population of the Island, and a good part of the rest of the state, was claiming to have seen it. The people who claimed to have been in The Retreat that night would not only have filled The Retreat; they would have filled the Astrodome and Rice Stadium, too.

Dino and I hadn't been there, though once or twice over the years I'd told people that I had been. The truth was that I would have been too young to get into The Retreat when the fight took place.

Hobart had been whipped, but not before tables had been wrecked, chairs smashed, and patrons walloped by accident.

A well-known state senator had gotten a black eye and a broken nose before he could get out of harm's way. Or maybe it had been a Hollywood B-movie star. Or a country singer who later had three number-one records in a row. Or all of the above. It depended on who was telling the story. Several people were supposed to have jumped from the windows into the Gulf to avoid getting battered in a similar fashion.

After that, Hobart never worked for the uncles again. According to the stories, he stayed on the Island, getting a job as a bouncer in a small club not affiliated with Dino's family. He might very well still be around, and it wasn't impossible that his old animosities had flared up. I'd have to ask Dino what he knew about him.

But right now I had a few other things to do. One was to see about retrieving a bullet or two from the old marine lab building.

After leaving Seawall Courts, I drove to the eastern end of the Island and parked in the same place I'd used the previous evening. The Mauser was wrapped in a towel under my seat. I took it out and stuck it in the waistband of my pants. This time, I wasn't going to take any chances. The Mag-Lite was still working, so I took it along as well.

It was even darker than it had been on my first trip to the building. I could hear the sea oats rippling in the breeze, and the lights in the condo windows stood out against the black sky.

I had the Mauser in my hand when I climbed the stairs, but this time there was no one in the building. I turned on the light and checked the floors near the walls, looking for pieces of flattened lead. I found one and pocketed it.

What I didn't find was shell casings. If whoever shot at me had been using an automatic, he'd come back himself and picked them up. I tried to remember how many shots had been fired and whether the shooter would have had time to reload a revolver. I found that I couldn't really recall. Then I remembered that the pistol had been silenced. Had to be an automatic.

I fingered the lead in my pocket. It was most likely too flat to do even an expert at ballistics much good. It would be next to impossible to check the lines and grooves. But I kept it anyway.

I searched the building even more thoroughly than I had before, looking for any proof that Harry had been there. I didn't find anything new. It was time to move on.

It was much too early to try getting into The Retreat, so I thought I'd talk to Dino. He was watching Larry King on CNN. Larry's guest was an actor I'd never heard of, and he was plugging a movie I had no plans to see. Dino would never see it either, but that didn't keep him from watching the interview.

He wasn't much interested in Alex Minor, but he did turn the set off when I asked him about Lawrence Hobart.

"The Hammer? I haven't thought of him in years. That was some fight he had with Braddy Macklin, though." When he mentioned the fight, he caught on. "You think he's mixed up in this?"

"Why not? Everyone else is. Do you know where he's living these days?"

"I don't even know if he's still alive. You want some Big Red?"

"Why not?"

Dino went to the kitchen, and I sat on the floral couch. When he came back in with the drinks, I asked if he could find out about Hobart.

"I've been thinking about that. There are still a few people around who'd know. I'll give 'em a call while you drink that stuff."

He handed me the glass and left the room. I drank it all before he got back.

"What did you find out?" I asked, setting the glass on a coaster on the coffee table.

"I found out that Hobart's still around. And he's been acting funny lately, too."

"Funny? He's doing comedy now?"

"No, and I don't think you oughta try it either, if that's your idea of a joke."

"Sorry. What's he been up to?"

"He's been talking to a lot of movers and shakers around town about the time when he worked for my uncles. Seems he's really interested in what the feeling is about having gambling come back to the Island."

"A hot topic," I said.

"Yeah. But he's against it."

That was interesting, but maybe Hobart had learned his lesson.

"Anyway," Dino went on, "Hobart can get into a lot of offices and homes because of his reputation. People remember him, and they'll listen to him whether they really pay any attention or not. Macklin was working for the other side. Maybe they tangled over that."

"Could be. So where's Hobart living these days?"

"Same place he's lived for the last thirty years. In one of those old houses on Avenue O." He gave me the address. "You oughta talk to him."

I wasn't eager to search The Retreat, and while I didn't think I'd enjoy talking to Hobart, he was a reasonable alternative.

"You want to come?" I asked as I got up from the couch.

"No thanks. You're the one getting paid for doing the work." He turned the TV back on.

I was almost out the door when the phone rang. Dino muted the TV and answered it, and I waited while he talked. I thought it might be some more information about Hobart, but I was wrong.

"That was Jody, from the bait shop," Dino said when he hung up.

"I thought the bait shop would be closed by now."

"It is. He's not there. He was calling from a pay phone at some place on Broadway."

"What did he want?"

"He says he saw Ro-Jo. He thought you'd want to know."

"Where is he?"

"Jody didn't know where he was heading. But he saw him walking along down by the cotton warehouses at the end of Broadway. Jody says Ro-Jo looked nervous, kept glancing all around him like he was being followed or something."

"Maybe he was just checking to see if the cops were around. Those warehouses might be a good place to get out of the weather. Maybe Ro-Jo was going inside."

"It might be hard to get over those fences."

"That's what makes it a good place," I said.

"You think maybe Harry could be there?"

"He could be anywhere. Or nowhere."

"What're you gonna do?"

I had a lot of choices. I could go to The Retreat, I could pay Hobart a visit, or I could scout out the warehouses. I didn't want to do any of those things, but at that moment going after Ro-Jo seemed to be the most likely way to get a lead on Harry's whereabouts. Besides, Ro-Jo had lied to me. I wanted to talk to him.

"I'm going to the warehouses," I said. "You want to come?"

"I didn't even want to go see Hobart," Dino said. "And that's legal. I'm sure not going in those warehouses."

"You'll miss all the fun."

Dino smiled. "I hope so," he said.

▽

18

THE COTTON WAREHOUSES at the bottom of Broadway had once been jammed with bale after bale of cotton that was shipped all over the world. The warehouses went on for blocks and extended far back from the street. There were probably miles of them, but they were all empty now.

Cotton was no longer the state's big cash crop. When I was a kid you could drive along the highways and see cotton growing in field after field, but these days it's not that way. You hardly ever see it, and whatever gets shipped must go out of Houston.

There were signs hanging on the gates of some of the warehouses, signs identical to the one I'd seen on the gates at the marine lab:

KEEP OUT
U. S. GOVERNMENT PROPERTY
TRESPASSERS WILL BE PROSECUTED

I was beginning to think that the government was the biggest property owner in Galveston.

But since the government was the people, that meant I was free to enter and do as I pleased. That's what I told myself, and it sounded just as false and hokey as it had when I'd tried it out earlier.

But what the hell. I had to tell myself something to justify what I was about to do, which was climb the fence and start searching the warehouses.

I parked the Jeep in the lot of a convenience store and

hoped they wouldn't have it towed. Maybe I'd be out before they even noticed the Jeep was there, though that didn't seem likely. There were a lot of warehouses to go through.

I didn't try the fence on Broadway, of course. There was far too much traffic and someone would have seen me for sure. They might not have reported me; in fact, I was pretty sure no one would even care. But I didn't want to take that chance.

Next to one group of warehouses there was a boarded-up building fronted by a large unlit parking lot with weeds growing up through the cracks in the concrete. I walked along the fence until I was at the back of the building, standing in the shadows it cast. It didn't take me long to get over the fence.

When I was on the other side, I pulled the Mauser from my waistband and took the flashlight from my back pocket. There was no need to turn it on just yet.

The first warehouse wasn't exactly a "house." It was long, empty, and open on both sides. I could see from one end of it to the other. There was no one there. I stepped up on the floor and turned on the light, sweeping it along to see if I'd missed anything. I hadn't.

I stood there for a minute, listening. All I could hear was the wind and the cars whishing along Broadway. I wondered how many bales of cotton this place might have held, and I thought about hot green fields, about the cotton pickers bent over as they moved along the rows dragging the long white cotton sacks behind them.

I walked across the floor and stepped down, then crossed a narrow, weed-filled area. The next warehouse was also completely open, and I found it as deserted as the previous one. The floor had been swept clean by the gulf breezes; there wasn't even a sign that a rat or a mouse had ever been there.

I walked through another open warehouse just like the first two before I came to one that was partially enclosed. One end was open, but the other was protected by sheet-metal walls.

I didn't announce my presence. I'd learned my lesson at the marine lab, not that it made any difference this time. There was no one hiding in the enclosed end of the warehouse. I was beginning to think that I was wasting my time, but there were plenty of warehouses left. I kept going.

Four or five warehouses later, I found Ro-Jo.

He was lying on the floor, and I knew he was dead as soon as I saw him.

The warehouse I was in was almost completely enclosed, and Ro-Jo was lying at the end nearest Broadway, where there were several cubicles that had probably served as offices of some kind, though they were empty space now. Shadows jumped all around as I shone the flashlight through the openings in their walls.

Ro-Jo was lying just outside the door of one of the cubicles, and his head was twisted unnaturally on his shoulders. I shined the light in his face. His lips were cut and swollen. Someone had hit him hard, and I wondered how much more damage would have shown up if he hadn't died before he'd had time to develop bruises.

His supermarket shopping cart wasn't far away. Somehow he'd managed to get it through the fence. The beam from my Mag-Lite sparkled off the cart's silvery wires. I didn't bother going through it. It didn't appear to have been disturbed. Whoever had killed Ro-Jo wasn't interested in the cart.

And whoever had killed him hadn't used a pistol. He'd been beaten and his neck broken. I wondered if he'd told his killer how to find Harry or whether he'd lied as he'd lied to me.

Or maybe he hadn't lied to me. Not exactly. Maybe he'd wanted me to go to the marine lab because that was where he'd told the others to go. Maybe he'd hoped I could stop them.

If that was true, he'd been very wrong. They hadn't found Harry, but they'd found Ro-Jo again. And this time they'd killed him.

I tried not to feel guilty about that, but feeling guilt is one of the things I do best. If only I'd done better at the lab, Ro-Jo might still be alive.

On the other hand, he might still be alive if he'd told me the truth in the first place. It was too bad he hadn't trusted me enough to do that. He wasn't going to get a second chance, and I was more convinced than ever that if I didn't find Harry before the other lookers did, Harry wasn't going to survive for long.

I didn't know whether to tell Barnes about Ro-Jo or not, but I supposed I had to. I couldn't just let the body stay where it was until someone else stumbled across it.

I turned to leave, and I'd taken two steps when I heard a noise behind me. I started to turn, but I wasn't fast enough. There was a step behind me and something hit me hard, square in the right kidney.

I dropped both the flashlight and the Mauser. The light went skittering across the floor, and the Mauser flew about six feet through the air, hit, and bounced twice. I landed on my knees, which didn't do either of them any good.

I was hit again, in the head this time, before I had a chance to react. I pitched forward, rolled, and tried to come to my feet. I might have made it if my right knee hadn't collapsed underneath me.

When I struck the floor this time, I rolled to my right and kept on rolling on the pitted wooden floor. I was hoping I could get to the Mauser, but my attacker was quicker than I was. He kicked it out of the way and then aimed a kick at my head.

He was not only bigger than I was, he was a lot quicker, and that was all I could tell. I couldn't see what he looked like because he had on a ski mask. I could see his foot, though. It looked like an aircraft carrier as it flew toward my head.

I tried to grab it, like hotshot private eyes do in the movies, but it was coming too fast. I barely managed to deflect it so that it missed most of my head, though it nearly took off my ear. I also felt a popping in my left little finger and then a sharp pain, as if the finger had been dislocated.

My attempt at self-defense did throw my attacker off balance, and he stumbled forward and almost tripped over me. I tried to help him along with a friendly shot to the groin.

Neither one of us had made much noise up until that point, but when I connected with his crotch, he let out a loud moan and went flailing into the shopping cart, which rolled into the wall of one of the cubicles before he was able to dislodge himself. There was a ringing noise as he kicked the cart away.

Meanwhile, I was looking for the Mauser. I saw a dark lump on the floor and made a dive for it. My fingers closed around the butt, and I brought it up to fire, but my assailant was gone.

The shopping cart was lying on its side near the doorway to one of the cubicles, and Ro-Jo's possessions were scattered on the floor. I was pretty sure that Ro-Jo's killer was inside the cubicle, where he'd been hiding when I entered. Now he was just waiting for me to make a move.

I decided to oblige him. I fired a shot at the wall.

The Mauser isn't a .45, but its cartridges have enough power to send a bullet through a wall if the wood isn't too thick. This wood wasn't. The bullet whacked through, and the echo of the shot rattled off the sheet-metal walls.

The man inside the cubicle had a gun. I'd been hoping he was unarmed, but apparently he'd just been trying to keep things quiet. Now that I'd started the shooting, he was no longer shy.

I saw the dark outline of his head and then he fired off two quick shots, both of which missed me. One of them hit the flashlight, however. It hit the lens instead of the barrel, and the warehouse was plunged into darkness.

▽

19

I WAS MOVING almost before the light went out, and I assumed that the man in the cubicle was doing the same. I popped off a round in that direction just to keep him awake, but I wasn't sure that I hit even the wall. It was so dark that I had no idea what was in front of me.

He fired back at my muzzle flash, but I was five feet away by that time and able to return his fire. I missed again, and the bullet pinged through one of the sheet-metal walls of the warehouse.

Then there was a sound like rattling thunder, and I thought for a second that a storm had hit, but it was only my big friend, who had crashed into the wall my last bullet had gone through.

He was blundering around in the dark like a bull rhino. I decided to join him.

My knee held up long enough for me to stand, and I started toward where I thought the killer might be. Sure enough, we ran into each other, and each of us made a grab.

He won. He got both arms around me and started to squeeze. I still had the Mauser in my right hand, and while I couldn't direct it at a vital spot, I could still pull the trigger.

The pistol was pointed straight down at the floor, and it was very close to the killer's leg. The muzzle flash burned him, as the bullet buried itself in the floor, and he relaxed his grip long enough for me to bend my knees and spring upward, banging the top of my head into his chin.

His teeth clicked together and he let me go, stumbling

backward into the wall again. I thought of shooting, but I was afraid I might actually hit him, not that I would have minded wounding him. I didn't want to be responsible for his death, however, no matter what he'd done to Ro-Jo. That kind of rough justice wasn't in my job description.

He rebounded from the wall, and either by accident or design ran right into me like a blitzing linebacker.

I hit the floor hard, the air whooshing out of my lungs. My head bounced once, and there was a bright flash behind my eyelids. For a second I thought that the lights had come on. They hadn't, of course. I lay there as limp as a string and waited for whatever was coming next, a foot in the face or a bullet in the brain. Whatever it was to be, there wasn't a thing I could do about it.

What happened was that a door opened and shut, leaving me alone in the warehouse with Ro-Jo's body lying not six feet from me. I knew that the killer was getting away, and I wished there was something I could do besides lie there on the floor, but I couldn't think of a thing.

My head didn't feel as if it was attached to my body, and I wondered if that was a bad sign. I didn't want to think about it, so I thought about fishing and how good it felt to hook a flounder in the bay or a speck from the dock. My head began to hurt a little less.

I kept on thinking for a while about fishing, about Cathy Macklin, about Harry, and eventually I discovered that there was something I could do besides just lie there and think.

I discovered that I could go to sleep. So I did.

I don't know how much time passed before I woke up. Probably not long, maybe fifteen minutes, maybe a little more. I was feeling much better. My head was feeling attached to the rest of me again, which was good in one way but bad in another. It made me aware that I was feeling pain in a lot of places where I had never felt pain before, from my hair to my toenails. I told myself that the pain would pass.

Most of it did after another fifteen minutes or so, and I

was able to sit up. I was even able to find the Mauser, which I stuck back in my waistband.

After that I crawled around the wall, trying to find the door. I was slow, but I was careful, and I finally found it. I pulled myself up on the frame, opened the door, and stepped outside.

I stood in the cold air and took stock of myself.

There was a knot on the back of my head, but it was hard, not soft. I took that as a good sign.

My head was pounding, sort of like the drumbeats in "Peggy Sue." That wasn't a good sign, but it wasn't a bad one.

My ear was painful to the touch and seemed to have a fever. That wasn't so bad either. At least it was still attached to my head.

My little finger looked like a cup handle. I grabbed the end and pulled as hard as I could. It popped back into place with no more pain than I might have felt if someone had hit it with a hammer.

I congratulated myself for not yelling and told myself that I had nothing to complain about, at least not compared to someone in Ro-Jo's condition.

Thinking of Ro-Jo reminded me of something. Leaving the door open, I went back inside the warehouse. There was enough light coming in from the outside to allow me to locate the Mag-Lite. I pocketed it and left.

The trip back over the fence was a lot harder than the first one had been, but I was walking more or less normally by the time I got back to the Jeep.

There was a pay phone next to the convenience store, and I used it to call the police. I didn't ask for Barnes or mention my name. I just reported the body in the warehouse. I could talk to Barnes later. Maybe. Hey, what had he done for me? I certainly didn't have time for him right at the moment. There were places to go and things to do.

* * *

Lawrence Hobart, aka the Hammer, lived in a house that was typical of those in its neighborhood: peeling paint, bad roof, more dirt in the yard than grass. It was up on blocks in case of flooding, and the porch was a good four feet off the ground. I could see a light through one of the front windows, so I supposed Hobart was home.

If I was lucky, he'd be panting and at least a little bruised, but I didn't think that would be the case. I'd hate to think that a man in his seventies could run over me like that.

I climbed the tall steps and knocked on the door. It was opened by a man who looked a little like Braddy Macklin must have looked before he was killed, sort of like Charles Atlas gone slightly to seed and wearing a bad hairpiece. Hobart had less gray in his hair than I did, but at least my hair was my own.

"What do you want?" he said, looking at me with narrowed eyes.

"Lawrence Hobart?" I said.

"Who wants to know?"

"Truman Smith. I have to talk to you."

"Bullshit you have to talk to me."

He was shutting the door as he spoke, but I put my shoulder into it and slammed it open, knocking him backward a step or two. He definitely wasn't the guy who'd run over me.

"Get your ass outta here or I'll call the cops," he said.

"Good idea. Ask for Gerald Barnes. Tell him to put a little hustle in it."

He thought about that and decided that calling the cops might not be such a good idea.

"I was a few years younger, I'd whip your ass," he said.

"I don't doubt it. Right now, your grandmother could probably do the job with one hand."

"Yeah, you don't look so good. What the hell you want, anyhow?"

"You know who I am?"

"Hell yes. You're that snot-nosed little fart used to hang around with Dino. Still do, from what I hear."

"Could you shut the door?" I said. "It's cold in here."

"Don't like to waste money on heat," he said, but he shut the door.

"Thanks," I said. "I've had a rough night."

"Yeah, it looks that way. What happened to you?"

"I tripped on a rug. You wouldn't happen to have an ibuprofen tablet, would you?"

"What's that?"

"Never mind. How about an aspirin?"

"Never touch the stuff."

"I have a pretty bad headache," I said.

"Big deal. You're a young guy. You can take it." He gave me a crooked smile. "What'd you want to talk about?"

"Gambling," I said, hoping he was right about my ability to take the headache. "Also Braddy Macklin. And Patrick Lytle."

The smile disappeared when I said Macklin's name. I was glad Hobart wasn't twenty years younger. Or even ten. He could have mopped the floor with me even if I'd been at my best.

"I don't know anything about those topics," he said.

"Sure you do. I'm old enough to remember that fight you had with Macklin. Anyone who's lived on the Island for over a month has heard that story. And gambling? I know what led up to that fight. You had a habit."

His brow furrowed, and he looked at me as if he might like to dismember me. I hoped he wouldn't try it. I didn't want to get hurt. After a second or two, his brow smoothed out, however, and the fire in his eyes dimmed. I let myself relax.

"Damn right, I had a habit," he said. "Now it'd get me a spot on one of those TV talk shows. Gambling addiction, they call it. Everybody would feel sorry for me and try to get me some help. They even got a hot-line number on the back of the lottery tickets. You can call if you got a problem. Back in the old days, nobody cared. They figured if you couldn't control it, you were just stupid, or weak. They didn't know it was an addiction. They got twelve-step programs for that kind of thing now."

I wondered if he watched the same shows Dino did. It sounded like a distinct possibility.

"What about Patrick Lytle?" I asked.

"Don't know him."

I winced as a particularly good drumbeat split my head. I'd switched from "Peggy Sue" to Sandy Nelson slamming the skins on "Teen Beat."

"Try again," I said. "Lytle's wife was a good friend of Macklin's, a very good friend. Don't tell me you didn't know about that."

"Maybe I remember a little about it, now that you mention it. It's all ancient history."

"Not to me. I thought maybe you could tell me a little about her."

He thought that one over. "You wanna sit down?"

He didn't have to ask me twice. The room we were in was furnished in early Salvation Army Thrift Store, and I sat on a sofa older than Dino's, if not in nearly as good condition. The foam rubber showed through several holes in the fabric. Hobart sat in a platform rocker that had a bed pillow in it in place of its original cushion.

"She was a real looker, Miz Lytle was," he told me after he'd settled himself. "Red hair. I always liked red hair on a woman. And real white skin, with a freckle or two. I don't mind freckles. Lots of red-haired women have 'em."

That wasn't exactly an earth-shaking revelation. I asked him about her gambling habits.

"She gambled, all right. Her husband, too."

Sally West hadn't remembered Lytle's gambling. Or maybe she hadn't known. What I was looking for was a way to explain how Lytle had lost his money.

"Big losers, were they?"

He shook his head. I thought I saw the hairpiece move, but I could have been wrong. My head still wasn't quite right, and it might have been affecting my vision.

"Nah," he said. "They were big winners. At least she was. I couldn't say about him."

"I didn't know there were ever any big winners at the uncles' tables," I said.

He got a faraway look. "Sometimes there were. It could be managed, especially if they were good-looking women that Braddy Macklin liked a whole lot."

I was shocked—shocked!—to discover that there might have been rigged gambling at The Island Retreat.

"Do you have any idea how much she might have won?"

The faraway look faded. "That was a long time ago. A damn long time."

"It was. But I think you can remember."

"OK, maybe I can. It was a lot. Not all at once, but over a year or so she took a lot of money out of The Retreat. Probably never spent a penny of it, either. No need to. She had two men taking care of her."

"But you don't remember about Lytle?"

"I didn't pay attention to him. I always had a weakness for a red-haired woman, and if there's one thing I don't blame that son of a bitch Macklin for, it's taking her away from her husband. He was a spineless little bastard anyway."

I tried to get Hobart's mind off the woman. "About Lytle's gambling . . ."

"Dammit, I told you I didn't pay any attention to him."

"He wasn't a winner, then."

That puzzled Hobart for a second, but then he got my point.

"You're right," he said. "If he'd been a winner, I'd have known about it. There weren't too many of 'em."

"Would Macklin know?"

"You trying to get smart with me? I know that asshole's dead, and I don't give much of a damn one way or another."

"Seen him lately?"

"What's that supposed to mean?"

"You and he were both talking to people about bringing gambling back to the Island. Except that you were on opposite sides. You must've crossed paths."

"Well, we didn't. I haven't seen that son of a bitch in thirty years. Never wanted to. I'll see him one more time, though. Wouldn't miss his funeral for the world."

"Were you talking to people about gambling because you oppose it on moral grounds, or were you working for someone?"

"That's none of your business, is it."

It wasn't a question, and I didn't feel like arguing the point. My head hurt too much. I stood up.

"I can find out," I said. "I can find out if you've seen Macklin, too."

He sat in his chair and looked at me. "Go ahead and find out. I don't give a damn."

Maybe he didn't. I left him sitting there, another old man who hadn't escaped the past. He could call it ancient history, but it still meant something to him, just like it meant something to most of us in one way or another. I was pretty sure it had a lot to do with Harry and Braddy and what had happened to both of them.

But Hobart was still a tough old buzzard, and he wasn't going to tell me any more than he already had, not without some powerful coercion. I didn't feel like coercing anyone. I just felt like going home and taking a long, hot shower and getting into bed.

I let Hobart's screen door slam behind me as I left. I walked down his steps to the Jeep and drove home.

▽

20

OF COURSE I couldn't go home and take a shower and go to bed. Or I could have, but that wasn't on the program yet. I had something else to do first. I had to go to The Island Retreat.

I'd entered two different deserted buildings in the last two nights, and I'd been beaten up and shot at both times. As a result, I'd developed terrific headaches. The one I had now had switched from "Teen Beat" to the intro to "Pipeline" by The Chantays.

I stopped at a convenience store and bought a bottle of ibuprofen and a can of Big Red to wash a couple of the tablets down with. I sat in the parking lot for a while after I'd finished the soda, and my head eventually began to feel better. I wasn't sure whether to credit the ibuprofen or the soft drink. I've often thought that Big Red might have secret curative powers. Maybe there had been an article on the subject in *Weekly World News*. If there hadn't been, there probably would be.

I drove to the seawall and parked the Jeep well down the street from The Retreat. I walked past a restaurant and a gift shop, both closed. The gift shop had piles of conch shells protected behind chicken wire on either side of its entrance. No one had ever found shells like that around Galveston.

Near the gift shop was a set of concrete steps built into the seawall. I went down the steps and walked along the narrow strip of beach to The Retreat.

Third pole on the west side, that was what Ro-Jo had said. I'd have to wade a little, but not much.

Thinking about what Ro-Jo had said to me reminded me that he was dead. Maybe because of the bump on my head, I hadn't really accepted that fact, in spite of seeing his body on the floor or even calling the police.

If there was ever anyone who didn't deserve to die like that, Ro-Jo was the one. He was just a simple guy who liked to keep to himself. Maybe he lived what politically correct people liked to call an "alternative lifestyle," but he didn't bother anyone. He just pushed his shopping cart and kept out of the way. I hoped I'd be able to find the person who'd killed him. Maybe I should have tried harder to shoot him when I'd had the chance.

I waded out into the Gulf until it was lapping around my calves. I could feel it sucking at my shoes as it pulled back from the shore. The water was cold, but not so cold that I couldn't stand it.

I didn't feel a lot like trying to climb up the pier leg Ro-Jo had recommended, but there were cross braces at easy intervals. If Harry could climb it, so could I.

Of course, I didn't have any proof that Harry had climbed it. I was just taking Ro-Jo's word for that.

I grabbed the first crosspiece and pulled myself up. My wet jeans stuck clammily to my legs, and the breeze from the Gulf turned everything below my knees into an icicle. Luckily, it didn't take me long to get to the top of the pier.

I could see the lights of the occasional car passing along Seawall Boulevard, but no one could see me. I was just a part of the pier. Or so I hoped.

I wrapped one arm around the pole I was hanging on to and pounded on the floor of The Retreat with my right hand. At first I thought I was going to have to climb right back down, but then I felt something give.

I pushed up and a section of floorboard moved. After that it was easy. I shoved the board aside and pulled myself through the space I'd made. In a couple of seconds I was sitting on the floor of The Retreat, my legs dangling down underneath.

It was even darker in The Retreat than it had been in the warehouse, if that was possible. I wished I had the Mag-Lite.

I pulled the Mauser out of my waistband, and for a few minutes I just sat and listened. I could hear the Gulf swirling under the pier, the wind blowing around the old building, and the cars on the street. That was all.

Of course I hadn't heard the guy in the warehouse either, but somehow The Retreat *felt* empty. It was an almost spooky feeling, as if I were alone with the ghosts of the uncles and their laughing customers. I could imagine the spinning roulette wheel, the clang of the old slots, the rattling of dice. Or maybe that was just my headache. I pulled my feet inside the building and stood up.

I tried feeling my way around. There was nothing in the room with me, no furniture of any kind. That wasn't surprising. This would have been the main entrance. The tables would have been farther back. I wasn't sure whether Macklin had been shot here, but I thought not. And that was why the cops hadn't found the loose floorboard.

I'd found it, but I don't know what else I had expected to find, except maybe Harry.

He wasn't there, however.

No one was.

I fumbled and stumbled through a couple of the other rooms, but I found nothing of importance. I couldn't see well enough, though there was a little light coming in through cracks around the boards that covered the windows.

Before I left, I sat on a chair covered with a plastic drop cloth and tried to make some sense of everything that had happened and that I'd learned since Dino found me on the fishing pier.

Nothing came of the effort. My head was throbbing too hard. Preston Epps was doing "Bongo Rock."

I went back to the front of The Retreat, dropped down through the hole, and climbed down to the beach.

Now I could go home.

When I woke up the next morning, Nameless was standing on my chest, looking me straight in the eyes. He'd probably sneaked up there to suck my breath, as cats are reputed to do, but I'd cleverly foiled him by waking up.

"I'm onto you," I said.

He started purring. He'd always been good at playing innocent, though he'd never managed to *look* that way. I shoved him off my chest and got up.

That was my first mistake of the day. When my feet touched the floor, a shock ran through my legs, up my torso, through my neck, and right to the top of my head. I touched the knot on the back of my head. It didn't feel any bigger than it had the night before, but it didn't feel any smaller either. My ear wasn't quite as tender, however.

I fed Nameless, which caused even more purring, and I decided he would never suck my breath. If he killed me, who'd feed him? Dino might, but Nameless couldn't count on that.

I hoped Nameless could reason that out for himself. I'd read somewhere that a cat had a brain the size of a marble. That didn't allow a lot of room for reasoning capabilities.

I cleaned up and went for a run. It was going to be a nice day. The rain was gone, the sun was bright, and the gulls were sailing overhead, hoping that I might have a couple of Chee-tos or something equally wonderful to toss to them. I didn't, but they occasionally glided down close to me just to make sure, begging and squalling.

I liked the sun and the gulls, so it was too bad that every other step I took threatened to cause the top of my head to go flying off. I ran only a couple of miles and went back to the house. There was no need to torture myself.

I ate some cereal and read the newspaper. There was no

mention of Ro-Jo, but it was a Houston paper. Houston doesn't report much Galveston news.

I went back to the bedroom and set the CD player to shuffling the Elvis discs. Elvis started in on "I Need Your Love Tonight" while I tried to do a better job of sorting things out than I had the previous evening. It was a little like trying to work a fifteen-hundred-piece jigsaw puzzle with no picture to guide me, but I kept it up until some things began to fall into place.

One thing was certain: Harry had disappeared. Ro-Jo, who was now dead, had told me a couple of places Harry might be, but Harry wasn't there. I'd probably never know, now, whether Ro-Jo had steered me to those places because he really believed Harry might be there, or because he'd steered someone else there and thought it might be fun if the two of us got together. I guess it didn't matter much.

The next thing I knew for sure was that someone else was looking for Harry. The question was why. Had Harry witnessed the murder of Braddy Macklin? If that was true, and it seemed to be at least a good possibility, then my question was answered.

But that brought up another couple of questions. Who had killed Macklin? And why?

And how was Patrick Lytle mixed up in all this? He said he wanted to find Harry, but his reasons didn't impress me. What about his wife and her gambling winnings?

And then there was Lawrence Hobart, working to keep gambling from returning to the Island. Who was he working for? As Macklin's old enemy, he had a good enough reason to kill him, but had he? He seemed mean enough.

Alex Minor was another question mark. I suspected that he represented the interests Dino's uncles had successfully kept off the Island while they were running things, but what if I was wrong about him? What if he was really what he said he was? Stranger things had happened. Not to me, however.

I had watched for him last night, but I'd never had the sense that I was being followed. Of course, it could have been

Minor in the warehouse. He might have gotten there ahead of me. Ro-Jo's killer was big enough to be Minor, but for some reason I didn't think Minor was the man I'd fought.

What really worried me was the question of whether Dino was being straight with me. Wouldn't he be the logical person to bring back gambling? Surely he must now and then feel a little stirring of memory and desire when he thought about what his uncles had meant to the Island. Was he the one who'd been backing Braddy Macklin?

Added to all that was the nagging feeling that somewhere in all of this there was something I'd missed, some connection that would clear things up a little if I could just pin it down and look at it.

Naturally, I couldn't.

All that thinking made my head hurt even more. Even Elvis singing "Don't" wasn't helping. I turned off the CD player and went back into the kitchen. I hadn't read the comics yet. Maybe "Calvin and Hobbes" would inspire me.

Or then again, maybe not.

▽

21

I DECIDED TO go in to work. I'd missed check-in day, which meant that there might not be too much to do. And maybe Zintner would know something about all the people I'd met and talked to, something that would help.

Besides that, I wanted to use the computer.

The office was already thick with smoke when I got there. I wondered if the Surgeon General was right about secondhand smoke. I hoped not.

There were two clients talking to the clerks. One of the clients was actually smiling as he told Betsy about his troubles with the police. He probably wouldn't think it was so amusing when Zintner had finished with him.

Nancy wasn't occupied, and she came over to my desk when I turned the computer on.

"Looking for someone?" she asked.

I admitted that I was.

"I didn't know that anyone had skipped out," she said.

I looked over my shoulder at Zintner's office and put my index finger to my lips.

Nancy leaned down and whispered, "A little private snooping?"

I nodded as I ran my fingers over the keyboard.

"Anyone I know?" she asked.

"Probably not," I said. "I'm just trying to find someone for the fun of it."

The idea of looking for someone for fun didn't appeal to

Nancy, and she went back over to her desk. Then I got to work in earnest.

The big-three credit bureaus have information on practically every adult in the country, and thanks to the fax modem we have an easy way to get in touch with them. I was curious about Laurel Lytle. If I could, I was going to find out if she was still alive. So I faxed my request to all three credit bureaus, explaining that I was a private investigator and assuring them that I wanted the file for legitimate purposes.

It took a while, but I eventually found out that if Mrs. Lytle was alive, she didn't have a credit rating. That didn't really mean she was dead, however. She could have remarried. She could have taken her maiden name back after leaving her husband. It could also mean that she'd never applied for credit.

There were other things I could do, starting at the county courthouse down the street. I could check birth records there, along with Laurel's marriage license. And I could find out her Texas driver's license number with the computer. I could also check some bank records, and maybe that way I could get a Social Security number; with that, I would bet I could find her anywhere.

I was about to leave and start on some of those things, but at that point Dale Becker came into the building.

He was walking just a little gingerly, but that wasn't what gave him away. What gave him away was my sudden memory of the way the man in the warehouse had groaned when I clubbed him in the groin.

He'd sounded a lot like Dale Becker.

Becker probably hadn't expected to see me in the office. I'd told him and Zintner that I was going to be taking some time off to look for Harry. After a quick glance in my direction, Becker ignored me and headed straight for Zintner's office.

I got up and put myself in front of him.

"Get outta the way, Smith," he said.

He put a big hand on my chest and pushed. He moved me, but he didn't move me far.

"That's a pretty nasty bruise on your chin," I said. "Fall down in the bathtub?"

He shoved me again. "I said get outta my way."

"You son of a bitch," I said. "You killed Ro-Jo."

He dropped his hand and backed up. "I didn't kill anybody. Now move it."

"What the hell's going on in here?" Zintner said behind me.

I turned my head and started to tell him, but I heard Nancy scream, and that's when Becker hit me.

Or that's when he tried. Nancy's scream gave me enough warning to pull away, though Becker's fist scraped my chin.

I snapped my head back in time to see his follow-up punch. His fist looked as big as a wrecking ball, and I ducked under it, grabbing him around the waist, pushing my head into his stomach, and bulldozing him backward.

Everyone was yelling by that time, and there seemed to be a lot of scrambling around, but I couldn't see anything but the floor.

Becker backed into a desk, but I just kept shoving. I had on my rubber-soled running shoes, so I had plenty of traction. The desk started moving backward, and I heard a chair fall over. Then I heard a crash that could only have been the computer. A wave of regret washed through me, but it was gone almost at once. It wasn't *my* computer.

By that time, Becker was getting his wits back, and he wrapped his arms around my chest and lifted.

He was a strong guy, and he had my feet off the floor almost before I realized what was going on. I lost my grip on his waist, and suddenly I was dangling upside down. Then he tried to drive me into the floor like a nail, except that I was going head first.

I got my hands down and broke the impact just as he released me. Before he could grab me again, I somersaulted forward and turned toward him.

He was coming straight at me, and as he tried to hit me

I got in a couple of quick punches to his bruised chin. As far as I could tell, his head didn't even move backward. Maybe I'd hurt the bruise. It was the best I could hope for.

He did a lot better, from his point of view anyway. He hit me squarely in the sternum, and all at once I was sailing backward, unable to catch my breath.

I hit one of the office's flimsy walls and felt it give behind me with a loud crack. At least I hoped it was the wall that cracked. It might have been my spine.

Becker came at me hard, so I did the only thing I could.

I kicked him in the face.

That got his attention. It also broke his nose. There was bright red blood streaming down his face, and he put up a hand to stop it.

I got to my feet and caught a breath, the first one I'd had in what seemed like a long time.

Becker looked at the blood on his hand and then at me. Yelling something I couldn't make out, he picked up a chair and threw it at me.

I ducked, but the chair hit me in the head, hard, and knocked me back into the wall. I slid down to the floor and closed my eyes, waiting for Becker to come and finish me off.

He didn't come, however. The next thing I knew, Nancy was fanning my face and asking me if I was all right.

I shook my head, an error of major proportions. For a short while there was a very interesting fireworks display behind my eyelids.

The next thing I heard was Zintner's tender voice yelling in my ear.

"Goddamn you, Smith, you've done ten thousand dollars' worth of damage in here in ten seconds. I'm calling the cops."

I tried to tell him I thought that calling the cops was a great idea, and that the entire building wasn't worth ten thousand dollars, but I'm not sure he got the message. I couldn't blame him. What I heard coming out of my mouth was more like "Thassa goo'dee."

"What's he saying?" Zintner asked Nancy.

She couldn't tell him, but that didn't matter. I tried to tell them my real concern.

"Get Becker," I said, or tried to say. I think it came out, "Gee'ber."

This time, however, Zintner got it. "That son of a bitch's long gone. You're gonna pay for this, Smith."

"My ass," I said. Or, "M'sss."

"You'll have to talk better than that," Zintner told me.

"You leave him alone," Nancy said. "Can't you see he's hurt?"

Zintner let her know that he didn't give much of a damn whether I lived or died, much less whether I was hurt, and I thought that was pretty small of him, especially considering what I knew. Or thought I knew.

Whatever that was, it would have to wait a while. I was fading in and out, and I wasn't going to be able to talk about it right then.

I tried to say something to Nancy, but I didn't get it out. I went to sleep instead.

I seemed to be doing a lot of that lately.

▽

22

I WOKE UP in a hospital room, which, if nothing else, proved that my hospitalization was as good as the agent who sold it to me had said it was.

My head wasn't hurting anymore, but then nothing was hurting. I wondered what they had given me.

I didn't wonder long. I just went back to sleep.

The next time I woke up, a nurse was in the room. She looked tough and practical and efficient. When she noticed I was awake, she asked how we were doing.

I told her that we were just fine.

She was glad to hear it and told me that Doctor would be in to see me later.

I explained that I didn't want to see Doctor. I wanted to get out of here.

She shook her head and told me there was no way I was leaving before Doctor saw me. I would have argued with her, but I didn't have the energy.

This time I didn't go back to sleep, which I hoped meant that whatever they'd given me was beginning to wear off. I started to turn on the TV set, which was hanging from some kind of attachment on the wall, but I was afraid that one of Dino's favorite talk shows would be on. I wasn't in the mood for macho bikers who had been kidnapped by space aliens and forced into sensitivity training. So I just lay in the bed and thought about things.

The more I thought, the more certain I was that I was right

about Becker. I reached for the telephone and called Dino.

When he answered, I could hear a talk show in the background, but I couldn't identify the host. As I told Dino what had happened, the sound from the TV disappeared, and I knew he'd hit the mute button.

"That bastard Becker," Dino said when I'd finished. "Are you gonna be all right?"

I said that I thought I was going to be fine, as long as I didn't get into any more fights.

"What're you gonna do about Becker, then?"

It would never have entered Dino's mind to call the police and report Becker. It had, however, entered mine, not that I was going to make the call. If Barnes had sent Minor to my house, Barnes wasn't my friend and I felt no obligation to him.

"I'll have to think about Becker," I told Dino. "Right now, there's something you can do for me."

"I'm not going after Becker for you, if that's what it is."

"I don't want you to go after anyone. I want you to call that real estate broker and find out if any locals are trying to make a deal for The Island Retreat."

"Why?"

"Because I want to know. It's important."

He said that he would make the call.

"Good. And there's one other thing."

"What's that?"

"I want you to tell me the truth right now. Are *you* trying to make a deal for The Retreat?"

"No." His tone showed that his feelings were hurt. "I thought I told you that."

"I just wanted to make sure."

"Well, you can be sure. I didn't have anything to do with anything. All I wanted you to do was find Harry. I didn't know that any of this other stuff was going to happen." He paused. "If you want out, I don't blame you. But I want you to know I was telling you the truth."

I thought that I believed him. "I don't want out. I just wanted to be sure. Call me back as soon as you know something." I gave him the room number. "If you have to threaten to kill somebody, go ahead and do it. I've got to know."

"Hey, I don't do stuff like that."

"There's always a first time," I said.

I hung up the phone and leaned back against the pillows. It was hard to be certain about what someone told you over the phone; it was better to be able to look people in the eye if you were trying to detect a lie. Nevertheless, Dino had sounded completely sincere. I hoped he was. And I hoped he would call me back soon.

He didn't. An hour dragged by, and then another, and I was about to call him again when Doctor showed up.

His name was Rodriguez. He was young and brisk and he told me that I had a concussion. He also said that they were going to keep me overnight for observation.

I didn't want to stay overnight, but that didn't bother Doctor a bit. He gave me any number of reasons why I shouldn't even consider getting out of the bed.

I told him that I knew all the reasons but that I was leaving anyway. And that I would be glad to sign a release relieving the hospital of all responsibility.

After about fifteen minutes of wrangling, he gave in and went to see about setting things up.

I was pulling on my pants when the phone rang. I held up the pants with one hand and answered the phone with the other. It was Dino.

"I bet you suspected this already," he said.

"Maybe I do, but I don't want to stand here all day while you confirm my suspicions."

"OK. There's a sort of syndicate of local investors looking into buying The Retreat. One of them happens to be your boss, and Dale Becker's. Wally Zintner."

That was exactly what I'd suspected. I wondered why

Wally hadn't just had Becker finish me off when they had the chance, while I was lying there on the floor of the bail bond office. Maybe there had been too many witnesses.

"Thanks, Dino. I'll talk to you later."

I started to hang up, but I could hear Dino yelling at me through the receiver.

"Don't hang up," he was yelling as I put the phone back to my ear.

"You don't have to yell," I said. "I can hear you."

"I want to know what you're gonna do now."

"Zip my pants," I said, and hung up.

After I'd signed all their forms, the hospital staff reluctantly released me on an unsuspecting world. I realized only after I was outside that I didn't have the Jeep. It was probably still at Zintner's building.

I went back inside the hospital and called AAA Bail Bonds. Nancy answered. When I told her who was calling, she asked how I felt.

"I'm fine," I said. "Would you mind coming to pick me up?"

"I suppose I could," she said. "It's nearly closing time."

"Is Wally still there?"

"He's here. He's not too happy with you right now."

"I'll bet. Tell him to wait there. I want to talk to him."

While Nancy was driving me back to AAA, I asked about Becker.

"He ran out after you went down. He hasn't been back."

"Has he called Wally?"

She told me that she didn't monitor Wally's calls. And she asked me what the fight had been about.

"Nothing much," I said.

"You men are all alike, so tough and macho. It wasn't nothing."

I admitted that maybe it was a little more than that.

"I heard you say Dale killed Ro-Jo. Who's Ro-Jo?"

"He was someone I knew."

"And you think Dale killed him?"

"Yes."

Nancy shook her head. "I don't think so," she said.

"Why not?"

"Dale likes to talk big, and maybe he even likes to get a little rough, but I don't think he would ever kill anyone."

I told her she felt that way because she sat in the same building with Dale all the time and didn't like to think a man who shared the same office space could be a killer.

"That's not it," she said. "Dale's really a gentle sort, deep down."

I laughed. "He was certainly gentle with me, all right. That chair was a really delicate touch."

"He only hit you because you were accusing him of doing something terrible."

I caught on then.

"You haven't been going out with Dale, have you?"

She blushed. "Once or twice."

"Case closed," I said.

She tried to get me to talk more about Dale and what he'd done, but I didn't have anything more to say on the topic, not until I'd talked to Wally Zintner.

Nancy let me out in front of the building. Everyone except Wally had already gone home, and she said she wasn't going to come inside.

"But you're wrong about Dale," she told me before she drove away.

I didn't think so. I thought Dale was a killer, even if I couldn't prove it. I went into the building, smelling the stale smoke as soon as I entered. The place didn't look much worse than usual, though the computer was a wreck. The monitor screen was gone and the case was cracked. I walked back to Zintner's little office.

He was sitting in his chair, his feet up on his desk. I could see that he was wearing his Tony Lama boots.

"You're a real troublemaker, Smith," he said, swinging his feet to the floor. "Old Dale's gonna be mighty pissed off at you."

"That's too bad," I said. "I guess you've already called the cops."

"Nope. Why would I do that?"

"Because Becker assaulted me. Right here in your building."

"You gonna press charges?"

"Oh, I'm going to do more than that."

Zintner looked up at me. He looked skinny and mean and dangerous.

"Damn," he said. "You're a real bastard, Smith. You know that?"

"I've been told that before."

"I bet. Sit down, will you? I don't like looking up all the time. Hurts my neck."

As much as I disliked his visitors' chair, I sat. I was still a little weak in the knees.

"That's better," he said. "Tell me something. What you got against old Dale?"

"He killed Ro-Jo," I said. "And he beat the hell out of me twice. And he's been shooting at me besides."

Zintner sighed. "Can you prove any of that, or are you just talking through your asshole?"

"I may not be able to prove it, but I know it. I'll be able to prove it sooner or later."

"Let's just start with how you know it. Why don't you explain that to me."

"Why would you care?"

"Well, old Dale's an employee of mine. Just like you are."

"Not just like me," I said. "And that's not why you want to know."

"All right," he said. "Why don't you tell me why I want to know."

"Because you're in on it with him," I said. "I can't quite

figure out why you killed Braddy Macklin, but I've got the rest of it."

"Damn," Zintner said, and then he chuckled. "I guess I might's well put my hands in the cuffs then, you being so smart and all."

This wasn't going exactly the way I'd planned it. Zintner was taking things far too calmly.

"Are you trying to tell me that you didn't know Becker was trying to find Harry Mercer? And that you didn't know he'd been shooting at me?"

"No," Zintner said. "I knew all about that."

"Then you know he killed Ro-Jo."

Zintner leaned back in his chair and put his Tony Lamas back up on the desk.

"That part," he said, "I'm not so sure about."

"You're admitting that Dale Becker shot at me, though? I've got that right?"

Zintner pretended to look around the room. Then he looked back at me.

"Any tape recorders in here?" he asked. "I don't see any, so I guess not. Yeah. I'm admitting he shot at you. But that doesn't mean old Dale would admit it."

"And that doesn't bother you? That he shot at me?"

"No," Wally said. "Hell no." He smiled. "Truth is, I don't blame him a bit."

▽

23

ZINTNER PULLED A package of unfiltered Camels from his shirt pocket and took a stainless steel Zippo off the desk. He flipped the lighter open, spun the wheel, and set fire to the Camel. Then he blew a long stream of smoke at the ceiling.

"Cat got your tongue, Smith?" he asked. He clicked the lighter shut and put it back on the desk.

I came out of my momentary trance. "You knew everything?"

Zintner nodded. "That's what I said."

"But not about Ro-Jo?"

"I knew about Ro-Jo being dead. I just didn't know about Dale doing the killing, and I still don't. He was there, sure, but he said he didn't kill anybody. And I think he's telling the truth."

I thought about what Dale had said when I'd confronted him that morning: "I didn't kill anybody."

"Why don't you tell me what you know?" I asked Zintner.

He inhaled, blew out smoke. "Tell you what," he said. "Let's trade."

"Trade what?"

"You tell me how you knew about me and Dale, and I'll tell you what I know about last night."

"And Saturday night, too," I said.

"All right. That too. It wasn't just that bruise on Dale's chin that put you onto him, was it?"

"No," I said. "There was a little more to it than that."

"So what was it?"

"It was that both of you knew I was looking for Harry when I came in the office on Monday. I should have wondered about it at the time, but I didn't. Dino wouldn't have told anyone that he'd hired me, and I sure hadn't told anyone. But you two knew it. While I was in the hospital today, I had time to think things over, and I figured out how you knew."

Not everything I'd said was strictly true, but it was close enough. Dino and I had told Cathy Macklin that I was looking for Harry, but I didn't think she moved in the same circles as Zintner and Becker. As it turned out, I was right.

"Dale was afraid you'd come up with it," Zintner said. "We were a little stupid about that."

"So was I. I shouldn't have called out my name when I was looking for Harry at the marine lab. What was Dale doing there, anyway?"

Zintner exhaled smoke. "Looking for Harry, just like you were."

I hadn't expected him to admit that, but then I hadn't expected him to admit any of the things he'd told me so far.

"Why was he looking for Harry?" I asked.

Zintner stubbed out his cigarette in a little glass ashtray that was already full of butts, probably a pack and a half's worth. And that was just from today.

"It's a long story," he said.

"I have time."

"All right. First of all, Macklin was working for me."

"I thought so. I know you're one of the investors who's thinking about buying The Island Retreat."

"I won't ask you how you found that out, but you had to dig. We've been trying to keep it a secret. Anyway, you're right. I think it's time for gambling to come back to the Island, and I think there's a lot of money to be made from it. There's plenty of opposition, like always, but I think this time the gamblers are going to win. And I wanted a part of the action."

"That's no reason to be looking for Harry," I said.

He got out another Camel and lit it with the Zippo. I sat and watched him smoke.

"You know Dale," he said finally.

I didn't know what that was supposed to mean, and I said so.

"Dale's got all kinds of snitches all over the Island. They like to tell him things."

"They tell him because they're afraid he'll beat the hell out of them. Like he did Ro-Jo."

"You want to hear this or not?" Zintner asked.

I said that I wanted to hear it.

"Then let's forget Ro-Jo for a minute. Like I said, Dale's got ears everywhere, and he heard that somebody had killed Braddy Macklin in The Retreat. The realtor had let me have a key to the place, and Braddy was checking it out for us. You know, see what kind of equipment was there, how much we'd have to spend to fix it up, that kind of thing. Somebody didn't like that, so they killed him."

"And Harry saw it."

"That's what Dale heard. But he couldn't find Harry. Now and then Ro-Jo told Becker things, but he swore he didn't know where Harry was. Said he hadn't seen Harry in a long time, but that there were places Harry used to hang out. That old lab was one."

"You know you've got competition for The Retreat?" I asked.

"You mean the boys from back East? Yeah. I know about them. You met Alex Minor?"

"I've met him."

"Well, then. You know the kind of people we're up against. We wouldn't want that in Galveston."

"You think Minor killed Macklin?"

"He's what you might call the logical suspect. He's about as hard to find as old Harry is, though."

"Have you told the police all this?"

Zintner laughed, coughed, and laughed some more. Then he crushed his Camel in the ashtray.

"Those things're gonna kill me someday," he said. "No, I haven't told the cops. After I find Harry, maybe I will."

"I thought you told me you were the policeman's friend."

"You knew better, though. Besides, I might be wrong. Minor might not have killed Braddy. I gotta be sure. Maybe there's somebody else in on this, somebody I don't know about."

I thought about Dino. Then I put that thought out of my mind. I also thought about Lawrence Hobart, but I didn't mention him, either. I wasn't going to tell Zintner everything I knew. I figured he wasn't going to level with me, either, not all the way.

"Assuming you're telling me the truth about all this, why did Becker try to kill me?" I asked.

Zintner smiled a thin, mean smile. "Now who says he was trying to kill you? Just because he took a few shots, that doesn't mean a thing. The way Dale told it to me, he was just trying to scare you."

Well, he'd certainly succeeded, but I wasn't going to give Zintner or Becker the satisfaction of admitting it.

"The way Dale tells it," Zintner went on, "he could have finished you off last night, but he didn't. At first, yeah, he was shooting at you. He thought you were the killer coming back to make sure Ro-Jo was dead or something. He didn't get a good look at you until you were out cold on the floor. When he realized who you were, he didn't try anything else. He just left you right where you were, sleeping like a baby."

I'd wondered why I'd survived. Now I knew. The man I'd tangled with—Becker—hadn't wanted to kill me. Or so Zintner wanted me to believe.

"When he was shooting, the bullets came awfully close to me."

"I told you: he wanted to scare you. He didn't know why you were looking for Harry. For all he knew, you were the one who'd killed Macklin." He smiled again. "We still don't know you aren't, not for sure."

"Let's say I didn't kill Macklin. And let's say Becker didn't. Then who killed Ro-Jo?"

"That's what we'd like to know. You didn't, not unless you were doubling back to check on the body, and Dale didn't. Who does that leave?"

Dale was big enough to have done it, but then so was Alex Minor. I hadn't seen Minor following me last night, but maybe he was ahead of me like everyone else seemed to be.

"Minor?" I said.

Zintner shrugged his narrow shoulders. "Could be."

"I think we should go to the police," I said.

Zintner didn't laugh. He just looked at me.

"All right, maybe that's not such a good idea."

"Damn right it's not. You and Dale might get thrown under the jail."

"We know a bondsman," I said. "He'd get us out."

Zintner smiled, and this time it wasn't so mean. "I don't think he'd take the risk."

"Look," I said, "my only interest in this whole thing is finding Harry. If I can do that, I'll forget the rest of it. We could work together."

"What you mean is that you want me and Dale to tell you everything we find out, but you won't tell us anything. Is that about right?"

It was, but I couldn't say that. So I said, "No. I'll cooperate."

Just like I was cooperating with Barnes.

"Tell you what," Zintner said. "Not that I don't trust you, but why don't we just go on like we are. Maybe you and Dale'll quit stumbling over each other. It doesn't matter which one of you finds Harry, just as long as one of you does."

It mattered to me, all right. I didn't want Harry to wind up like Ro-Jo had, but I don't think Zintner really cared one way or another. All he wanted was information, and if he couldn't get it from Harry, he'd get it some other way. And the truth was that I'd just about run out of places to look. I wanted the kind of information Becker could get from his collection of snitches.

On the other hand, I had a few things to work on that Zintner knew nothing about. Or that he hadn't said anything about. That didn't mean he didn't know.

"All right," I said. "We keep on working separately. But if Dale gets in my way again, he might get hurt."

"From the looks of you, I'd say you won't be hurting anybody for a while. By the way, Dale's sorry about the fight here in the office. He wouldn't have got into it with you if you hadn't pushed him."

I said, "Tell him that if it happens again, I'm going to pull that gold earring right out of his earlobe."

Zintner laughed and reached for his Camels. "Now there's a sight I'd like to see."

▽

24

WHEN I GOT home, the little red light on the answering machine was flashing. I ignored it and called Cathy Macklin in hopes that she might go out to dinner with me.

She told me that she didn't feel like going anywhere. She'd gotten word that the autopsy on her father was complete, and she'd scheduled the funeral for the next morning. I was sorry that she didn't feel like seeing me that evening, but the truth was that I wasn't feeling much like going out myself. I told her I'd see her at the funeral.

Nameless was rumbling around my legs as I talked, so I hung up and fed him. As soon as he gobbled his food, he wanted back out. He probably had a date.

After letting him out, I listened to my messages. There were three of them, and they were all from Patrick Lytle. He wanted to know whether I'd found Harry, why I hadn't called, and when he could expect to see me. I didn't feel like talking to him, so I erased the messages and listened to Elvis on the CD player while I read a few pages of *Look Homeward, Angel*.

I put the book aside after a few minutes because I couldn't keep my mind on what I was reading. I was too wrapped up in other things. And the thing that bothered me most was something about Lytle. I knew how Becker and Zintner had found out about my looking for Harry. That had been my fault.

But who had told Patrick Lytle?

* * *

There was to be no memorial service for Braddy Macklin, so the next morning a little before nine I drove the Jeep to the old city cemetery on Broadway. The cemetery predates the Civil War, and some of the headstones are faded now with time and age. There are soaring monuments topped with angels, too, and marble tombs streaked with rust-colored weather stains.

I drove through the gate at the 40th Street entrance and wound my way around until I saw a small group gathered near a mausoleum. There was a hearse parked nearby, and the name of a local funeral home appeared in one of its windows in tastefully small silver letters.

Braddy Macklin wasn't going to be buried, as it turned out. He was going to be entombed alongside his wife. On the Island you can't dig down very far before you hit water.

There were several people at the tomb when I arrived. They included Cathy Macklin, Gerald Barnes, and a man whom I supposed was the minister designated to say a few final words about Macklin. There were also two men in black suits who probably worked for the funeral home. All those were people I'd expected to see.

I hadn't expected to see Patrick Lytle and his grandson, Paul, however. They were there, not far from the hearse, Patrick in his wheelchair and his grandson standing right behind him. There was a smile of fierce satisfaction on the elder Lytle's face, as if he had waited years for what he was about to see. The grandson, on the other hand, looked completely detached, almost bored. He wasn't even watching the funerary proceedings; he was watching a white gull sailing through the intensely blue sky.

I hadn't expected Dino and Evelyn to be there, either, but they were, and after saying a few meaningless words to Cathy, I walked over to join them.

"I'm surprised to see you outside the house," I told Dino. "Isn't it about time for Donahue?"

"I got an obligation to Macklin," Dino said. "I had to be here."

"What obligation?" I asked.

Dino was about to answer, but Evelyn punched him in the arm and he hushed. The minister was talking. He had a soft voice, and we were standing far enough away that I couldn't quite make out all the words, not that the words mattered. I'd heard them all before. I listened to the cars passing on Broadway, the squeal of tires, the occasional horn honking.

The minister's words didn't take long. The tomb doors were closed, and the hearse drove away.

"What obligation?" I asked again.

"Macklin worked for the family," Dino said. "No matter what happened to him, he worked for the family. I stick up for the family."

Friends and family. Dino was big on things like that. Somebody said that nobody noticed when old men died except other old men. That wasn't true. There was always someone to notice and to care, even if it was someone like Dino, who cared for reasons that the dead man might not even have understood.

I said good-bye to Dino and Evelyn and walked toward the tomb. I was going to talk to Cathy again, but Barnes headed me off. I said hello and started to step around him, but he put a hand on my arm.

"How's the investigation coming, Smith?" he asked.

"What investigation?" I asked. I didn't want to talk to Barnes.

"Harry Mercer. You said you were looking for him."

"I was. I haven't found him."

"Yeah. I bet. And you don't have anything for me?"

I reached into the pocket of my jeans. "As a matter of fact, I do." I handed him the flattened piece of lead I'd picked up at the lab.

He rolled it between his fingers, hardly looking at it, and slipped it into his pocket.

"Did you find any casings?"

"No. Either the shooter was using a revolver or someone came back and picked them up."

I knew that the shooter had been using an automatic, and I suspected that I'd even seen the gun, in Zintner's desk drawer, though there hadn't been a silencer on it. Homemade silencers don't last long.

Barnes didn't really care about the casings at the marine lab. He had something else on his mind.

"I guess you wouldn't know a thing about Harry's friend Ro-Jo, either," he said.

"What about him?"

"Somebody killed him last night, in one of the old cotton warehouses."

I tried to look surprised. "Was he shot?"

"That's a good question, Smith. Let me put it this way: we found a lot of shell casings around. And because the place has a wooden floor, we found some slugs that are in a lot better shape than that piece of crap you just gave me."

I hadn't given any thought to the casings and slugs at the warehouse. I wondered if Becker had found the time to go back and clean his up. Probably not.

"We'll be sending them off for ballistics tests," Barnes said. "Does that bother you?"

"Should it?"

"I guess that depends," he said, "on whether some of them came from a certain Mauser that's been used around here before."

"You wouldn't be accusing me of anything, would you?"

"Not me. I'm just a cop doing a job. But if I find out that your gun was used in that warehouse, you're in big trouble, Smith."

"I didn't shoot Ro-Jo," I said.

"Hell, Smith, I know that. But that doesn't mean you didn't kill him."

I shook my head. "You're too slick for me, Barnes. I don't know what you're getting at."

"Maybe not," he said, as if he didn't believe a word of it. "But I wouldn't bet my house payment on it. See you around, Smith."

He walked away through the headstones, and I turned to look for Cathy. She was still standing at the tomb, but the Lytles were with her. I didn't want to talk to Patrick, though it appeared that I wasn't going to be able to avoid it.

When Paul saw me walking in their direction, he bent down and said something to his grandfather, who said a few more words to Cathy and then nodded to Paul. Paul turned the chair and pushed it toward me.

"Good morning, Mr. Smith," Patrick said in his wheezy voice. "It's a wonderful day for a funeral."

"I'm not so sure any day is a good day for that," I said.

Lytle raised his arms as if to embrace the day. His wide smile showed yellowing teeth.

"I haven't been outside in years," he said. "But this"—he looked toward the tomb—"this makes me wonder what I've been missing."

"Life," I said. "That's all."

"And death," Lytle said. "You must know, Mr. Smith, that there's nothing quite so satisfying as the death of an old enemy. I've waited years for this day."

"He's been dead for a while," I pointed out.

"Yes, but now he is finally and irrevocably entombed." Lytle was positively beaming. "I must say I find it quite gratifying."

"I'm glad you're so happy."

"Oh, I'm not happy about everything," he said. "I'm actually very disappointed in you, for example. I left you a number of messages."

"I got in late last night," I said. "I was planning to give you a call today."

"I'm sure you were. But what were you going to tell me? Have you made any progress in finding Mr. Mercer?"

I wondered if Harry had ever been called Mr. Mercer in his life. Most likely he hadn't, and certainly not by the likes of Patrick Lytle.

"I haven't found him," I said.

"Really, I'm most disappointed," Lytle said. "I do want to

help him, and I can't do that unless you bring him to me."

"I'll see what I can do," I told him. "Now I have a question for you."

"I'll be glad to tell you anything that might help, but I'm afraid I know nothing. I have very little contact with people on the Island, and I never leave my home."

"So you keep telling me. What I'd like to know is how you found out I was looking for Harry."

Lytle's old eyes clouded and he looked down at the blanket that covered his legs. His liver-spotted hands lay in his lap, and he turned them over slowly.

"I don't believe that's any of your business," he said after a second or two.

"It is, though. It might help me find him."

Lytle gave it some thought. "Very well. If you must know, it was your employer who told me. Wally Zintner."

Now that was interesting. If I could believe it.

"There," Lytle said. "I've told you. Is it going to help you?"

"I'll let you know," I said.

Lytle grunted. "I hope that you will. I dislike having to leave messages on those infernal machines." He gave me a hard stare. "Take me to the van, Paul."

Throughout my entire conversation with his grandfather, Paul Lytle had stood behind the chair, his hands resting calmly on the handles. He had appeared to be completely uninterested in our conversation, hardly even glancing at me or his grandfather. But he was listening, all right. He tipped the chair backward, turned it, and wheeled Patrick Lytle toward a maroon Chevy Astro van parked a little way from the tomb.

I watched them go, hoping to see Cathy Macklin, but she was no longer there.

▽

25

I WAS FEELING much better than I had after leaving the hospital. My head wasn't throbbing, and my ear wasn't swollen. I'd slept pretty well, too, and that had helped. It was also, as Lytle had said, a wonderful day. A front had passed through, and the humidity was probably somewhere around forty percent. It doesn't get that low on the Island very often.

The only disturbing element of the day, with the exception of the fact that I hadn't found Harry yet, was that Barnes was going to know very soon that I'd been firing my pistol in the cotton warehouse where Ro-Jo's body had been found. He already had the ballistics records from the time I'd looked for Dino's daughter; all he had to do was get a match with the slugs from the warehouse, which he certainly would.

I had two courses of action. I could tell the truth or I could lie.

Of the two, the latter was by far the most attractive.

I could claim that my pistol had been stolen in a break-in at the house where I was living. Barnes would, of course, ask why the burglary hadn't been reported, and I would say that I hadn't wanted to bother the police, who, I was sure, had more pressing things to investigate.

I could almost hear his reaction to that. It wasn't going to be pleasant, and the lie probably wasn't going to keep me out of jail.

So in spite of my strong inclination to the contrary, it seemed that I was going to have to tell the truth.

How embarrassing.

There was another option, which involved finding Harry and solving Ro-Jo's murder, thereby giving Barnes the whole case wrapped up in a nice little package.

If I could do that, he might go easy on me about the pistol. Besides, if he didn't find it in my possession, there was no way he could prove that I was the one who'd fired it.

The problem with that whole idea was that I didn't seem to be one step closer to finding Harry than I'd been the afternoon Dino found me on the pier.

I told myself that if I'd been better at my job, Ro-Jo would still be alive.

Then I told myself to shut up. I couldn't go on blaming myself for everything that happened, not even for what had happened to Jan. Some things happened in spite of what I could do, not because of what I had done. There was no way that Ro-Jo's death could have been my fault.

I was so convincing that I almost believed myself.

"Flounder," Jody said when I walked in the bait shop. "That's what you want to go for." He was talking too fast. "They be hittin' on a day like this, even if it is January. You go wadin'—"

I held up a hand to stop him. "I don't want to go fishing, Jody. You know what happened to Ro-Jo?"

He looked around the dimly lit shop. There was no one there but me and him. Outside the door, the sun fell warm and bright on the tiny parking lot.

"I heard 'bout it. I wish I hadn', though. I wish I hadn' called you, neither. I be sure enough sorry 'bout doin' that."

"I didn't kill Ro-Jo," I said. "You don't think I'd be here if I'd killed anyone, do you?"

"Hard to tell," Jody said. "Maybe you here to kill me now."

"You know better than that. What would I kill you with?"

"Folks say whoever killed Ro-Jo done it with his bare hands. Maybe you do it that way."

"You're bigger than I am," I said.

"That don't mean nothin'. Maybe you know that kung fu kind of fightin'."

"I don't know kung fu, and I didn't kill Ro-Jo. I'm not going to kill you, either."

He looked as if he still didn't quite believe me and as if he would be really happy if some other customer walked through the door so that he wouldn't be alone with me in the little shop.

"Look, Jody," I said, "this is all about Harry. He saw something he wasn't meant to see, and now someone's hunting him. Has anybody been in here asking about him?"

"Nobody 'cept you."

"I have to find him. I'm afraid that if I don't, he might wind up like Ro-Jo. You wouldn't want that, would you?"

"Harry never hurt nobody."

"That doesn't help much," I said. "Whoever killed Ro-Jo was trying to beat information out of him. Maybe Ro-Jo told him something before he died, if he knew anything to tell. If he did, Harry's in danger."

I was pretty sure I would have told whatever I knew if someone were beating me the way Ro-Jo had been beaten. Ro-Jo might have held out, and he might not even have known where Harry was hiding, but I couldn't count on that.

"I'd help Harry if I could," Jody said. "But I don't know where he's at. I'd help him if I could."

He was still acting skittish, as if I were a threat to him. I'd always thought of myself as a relatively harmless-looking guy. I wondered if I'd sprouted horns and a forked tail since I'd last checked the mirror.

"I believe you," I said. "But maybe someone else knows. Is there anyone you can think of who might have an idea where Harry is? It doesn't even have to be a good idea. Any old idea at all would help."

Jody's eyes slid away from me, and I was instantly certain that he did know something he wasn't telling.

"Jody," I said. "You've got to help me find Harry before someone else does. I'm not going to hurt him. You'd know that if you thought about it."

He turned back to me. "OK," he said. "There might be somebody who could help you."

Galveston has a number of mixed neighborhoods, but a lot of the black population lives just off Broadway in housing projects that are just as depressing to look at as any similar project anywhere in the country—drab brick apartments with clothes hanging on lines strung in the sterile yards. Now and then there's some evidence of a happier kind of existence, a bright plastic scooter or dollhouse that show their scuffs and dirt only when you get close to them.

There are usually people standing in streets near the projects, talking or leaning against the cars. Youth gangs are a problem in Galveston, and some of the young men you see in the neighborhood have beepers on their belts. Even some of the younger kids have them.

In the blocks near the projects there are houses and bars in varying degrees of repair. I was looking for a house not far from the cemetery and just a block from the railroad yards. There weren't a lot of white faces around. In fact, except for mine there weren't *any*. I felt a little conspicuous sitting in the uncovered Jeep.

I stopped in front of the house. Sometime within the last year or so it had been about half-painted a light blue, but for some reason the job had never been completed. The rest of the house was a weathered gray. There were rusted screens on the windows, but the yard looked good. No dark green winter weeds sprouted in it. Someone had taken care of the yard.

I could feel the eyes on me when I got out of the Jeep, and the only comforting thought I could muster was that if Alex Minor was following me, he was going to have a lot more trouble getting to the house than I was. I was the wrong color, but at least I looked as if I belonged on the Island. Minor looked more like he belonged in Houston, and on the Island that's not a compliment.

I climbed the cement steps and knocked on the screen door. It rattled in its frame.

I stood there for what seemed like a very long time. It was as if everything on the street had frozen in position. I looked around the neighborhood, but no eyes met mine.

Finally someone came to the door and pushed it open. I had to step down to get out of the way, and I found my eyes on a level with those of a very old woman. She might have been as old as Sally West. She might have been older.

She was very short and very thin, and her mouth was sunken as if she didn't have a tooth in her head. Her hair was white and pulled close to her head. She looked at me as if waiting for me to say something.

So I did. "Mrs. Williams?"

"Tha's me," she said. "Who're you?"

"Truman Smith. Did Jody phone you?"

"He phone me, say you comin'. Didn' say what you want, though. You gonna tell me that?"

I was getting more and more uncomfortable standing there with eight or ten people watching me and pretending not to.

"Could I come inside and tell you?" I asked.

"I don' know you. Don' know a thing about you. I'm jus' a he'pless ole woman. You ain' gonna come in my house to talk, no sir."

"All right," I said. I didn't want to argue. Someone might decide that Mrs. Williams needed protecting and come over. "We can talk here. It's about Harry. Harry Mercer."

She looked at me for a long time. Then she looked over my head and sort of nodded. The neighborhood unfroze. I could see movement out of the corner of my eyes, and I could hear voices.

"Maybe you better come in after all," Mrs. Williams said.

* * *

The little sitting room was as neat as the yard. There were even doilies on the end tables. There was a smoky smell in the air, but it wasn't the smell of cigarettes; it was a little like the smell of a fireplace or wood-burning stove, though I had seen neither in the house as I walked to the sitting room.

Mrs. Williams took a seat in a straight-backed wooden rocker that Sally West might have admired. I sat in a ladder-backed chair with a straw bottom.

"What you askin' 'bout Harry for?" Mrs. Williams wanted to know when we were seated.

I told her about Dino. Like everyone else on the Island, she'd heard of him, and also like nearly everyone else, she'd never seen him.

"Why he want to find Harry?" she asked.

"Harry's his friend. Dino likes things that remind him of the old days, and Harry's been around longer than anybody."

"Huh. Not no longer than me."

"Maybe not. But Dino thinks something may have happened to Harry, so he asked me to find him."

"Ain' nothin' happen to Harry."

"Do you know where he is?"

"No sir, I don' know. Where Harry is, tha's his business."

"Jody said you were Harry's friend."

"I guess you could say that. I been knowin' Harry Mercer since we was kids. But that don' mean he tell me ever'thing he knows."

"I'm worried about him," I said. "I'm afraid someone's going to hurt him if I don't find him first."

"If you can't find him, how you think anybody else gonna do it?"

"They might get lucky," I said.

"They might not, though. I know Harry's off the streets. I heard 'bout that. But I don' know why, and it ain' none of my business, no more'n it's yours. Why don' you jus' leave Harry alone?"

I told her again that I was afraid of what might happen and asked her if she'd heard about Ro-Jo.

"I heard. I hear a lot of things. You think the man got Ro-Jo's after Harry?"

"I'm pretty sure of it."

"Well, we jus' have to hope that he don' get lucky, 'cause I ain' able to he'p you."

"One other thing," I said. "Did Harry have a sister?"

That got a smile, and I could see that I was right about her teeth. She didn't have any.

"Harry had a brother," she said. "Fine-lookin' boy, he was. I remember him very well." She stopped smiling. "But he died right after the war. Harry never had no sister. Why you want to know that?"

I told her about Alex Minor.

"He sound like a bad man," she said.

"He is," I agreed. "And he's looking for Harry."

"He the one got Ro-Jo?"

"I don't know. He might be."

"Even if he is, don' matter. I still can't he'p you."

She leaned back in her chair and started to rock. I knew that the discussion was over, so I got up to leave.

"Mr. Smith?" she said as I started out of the room.

I turned around.

"If I fin' out anything, I get in touch with Jody. I don' want Harry to get hurt."

I'd hoped for more, but I'd settle for what I could get. I thanked her and went outside. There were still people in the street and in the yards, but no one watched me as I got in the Jeep and drove away.

▽

26

I TOLD DINO that it was much too early for lunch, but he insisted on fixing chicken pot pies, which he heated in a convection oven he'd ordered by calling an 800 number after watching an infomercial on cable.

"This thing is great," he said as the fan in the top of the oven whirred away. "Cooks a lot faster than a conventional oven, and it warms the pies all the way through. You don't have to take them out of the little aluminum pans, either. You oughta get you one, Tru."

"I hope you're not going to start watching those infomercials instead of the talk shows."

He didn't exactly blush, but he had the grace to look a little ashamed.

"They just come on late at night and on Sundays," he said. "You can get some neat stuff."

"Right. Like hair paint for your bald spot."

"OK, maybe everything's not so great, but what about that Flowbee?"

I told him that I didn't know what a Flowbee was.

"It's a machine to cut hair. You hook it up to your vacuum cleaner."

I held up a hand. "I don't want to hear this," I said.

He would have told me anyway, but there was a little *ding* from the oven that meant the chicken pot pies were ready. He set them in a couple of plates he'd already placed on the table and we sat down to eat.

The pies were hot, all right, but there was one drawback.

They tasted like chicken pot pies. I was sorry I hadn't insisted that we go out. Even worse, Dino had run out of Big Red for me to wash the pie down with.

"You'll have to bring a couple in the next time you come," he said.

I told him not to worry, that I'd be sure to do that. He tried to talk me into drinking a glass of Diet Coke, but I wouldn't go for it. I drank water instead.

When we'd eaten, Dino wanted to go to his living room and watch *The People's Court*. I told him that we needed to talk. He sighed, but we stayed in the kitchen.

After I'd finished telling him everything that had happened, he said, "You could have called me from the hospital. I'd have come after you."

He probably even meant it, though I don't think he would actually have done it. He might have gotten Evelyn to do it, however.

"It doesn't matter," I said. "What matters is what we're going to do."

"Let's go through the whole thing and see what we know for sure," he said. "Or what we think we know. Then we'll decide what we have to do next."

He meant that we'd decide what *I'd* have to do next, but there was no use in telling him that. So we talked everything over and tried to sort things out.

We knew that Harry had disappeared about the time Braddy Macklin was killed, and we thought we knew that Harry had witnessed Macklin's death and had somehow escaped.

We thought we knew that Macklin's killer was after Harry, and we were sure that Becker and Zintner were after him.

"You believe Zintner?" Dino asked.

"I believe he wants Harry. I'm still not sure *why* he wants him."

"Zintner wouldn't go to the cops." There was approval in Dino's voice. "If Macklin was working for him, he'd want to settle the score himself."

"You sound like you believe him."

"I'd probably do the same thing. And Becker didn't finish you off when he had the chance."

"Gee, that makes me like him even more than ever."

"You don't have to like him. Just give him the benefit of the doubt."

I was giving Dino the benefit of the doubt by going over all this with him. I'd decided that there were already enough suspects without having to distrust my oldest friend. I hoped I wasn't wrong.

"If we take Becker and Zintner off our list of suspects, who does that leave?" I asked.

"The Hammer," Dino said. "He's old, but he's probably still man enough to take out Ro-Jo."

"And why would Hobart kill Macklin?"

"Because they hated each other for over thirty years. Because they were on opposite sides when it came to bringing gambling back to the Island. With two guys like that, you don't need anything else."

I wondered *why* they were on opposite sides. I wasn't satisfied that Hobart was opposed to gambling on moral grounds. He didn't seem to me to be the kind of man who spent a lot of time worrying about the moral consequences of anything, much less gambling. His own addiction didn't seem to be the real reason, no matter what he said.

"Hobart was at home last night, taking it easy," I said. "Could he have killed Ro-Jo?"

"How long had Ro-Jo been dead before you got to Hobart's house?"

I couldn't answer that with any certainty. Ro-Jo could have been dead for an hour or two by the time I found him, and after finding him I'd been out of things for a while, lying on the floor of the warehouse.

"I get the point," I said. "Hobart could have done it. He had plenty of time to kill Ro-Jo and then go home and make himself comfortable before I was able to get to him. Who else do we have?"

"Alex Minor," Dino said. "I wasn't paying much attention when you told me about him the other day. I guess I should have been."

"I've been worrying about Minor," I said, wondering why he hadn't turned up. "I thought he'd be following me around, but I haven't seen any sign of him."

"Then don't worry about him until he shows up. Who does that leave?"

I mentioned Laurel Lytle.

"You think she's back in town? Nobody's heard from her in years."

"I don't know where she is. I can't find any trace of her, but I've got a few other places to look."

"Why would she kill Macklin?"

"I don't know. It's just that she seems like the loose end in all of this. Maybe there's something we don't know about their relationship. Do you remember her daughter, Mary Beth?"

"She was a little older than us," Dino said. "The guy with old man Lytle at the cemetery today, what's his name?"

"Paul," I said.

"Yeah. He's Mary Beth's kid. She left here right after high school and got married, but she's dead now. That's all I know."

That wasn't much help, and it certainly didn't tell me any more about Laurel. I'd have to do some more checking. And there was something else I didn't know. I was still unsure about who'd told Lytle I was looking for Harry. I mentioned that fact to Dino.

"I thought you said it was Zintner."

"Not exactly. I said that's what Lytle told me. The more I think about it, the less likely it seems. Zintner wouldn't tell anybody anything unless he thought there was something in it for him. If Lytle had called him, he would have tried to persuade him to use Becker. That way Zintner would get paid for a job he was already doing."

"But not you," Dino said.

"I told Lytle that I already had a client."

"Yeah. Well, if Zintner didn't tell him, we know who did."

Maybe Dino did, but I didn't. It wouldn't have been Barnes; Lytle wouldn't have called him.

"Who?" I asked.

"You're not thinking," Dino said. "Who else knew?"

Almost before he'd asked the question, I knew the answer, just as I should have known it all along. There was only one person it could have been.

Cathy Macklin.

"You were blocking it," Dino told me when he saw that I'd tumbled. "I could tell you liked her."

"Why would she tell Lytle I was looking for Harry?" I said. "What's the connection?"

"You're asking me? How would I know? You're the detective. You figure it out."

I didn't want to figure it out. Besides the fact that I felt as if I'd failed too often, there was another reason I'd stopped looking for people. Too many times things didn't work out the way they should have. Even when you made the right connections, even when you located the person you were looking for, you lost something along the way. I'd found Dino's daughter, all right, but Dino and I had lost a friend. Now it seemed that I might lose Cathy before I even got to know her. And she was the one I'd decided to trust.

"I'll have to ask her," I said.

There were a couple of other things I could ask as well. Like, how had Lytle known about the service at the cemetery that morning? It hadn't been in the papers. Even Cathy hadn't known until last night. She must have told him, which meant that they'd had more than one conversation. I didn't like the implications of that.

"Why don't you go talk to her?" Dino said. "I think I'll stay here and watch TV. I think Oprah's gonna have a pretty good show today. You can let me know what you find out."

I told him that I would.

▽

27

THE SUN WAS still shining when I drove to the Seawall Courts, but somehow the day didn't seem quite as bright as it had earlier. I really didn't want Cathy to be mixed up in the murders of her father and Ro-Jo, but it was beginning to appear that she might be.

As I climbed the stairs to her apartment, I thought about her behavior at the cemetery. It was almost as if she had been avoiding me. Could the presence of Lytle have had something to do with that?

She answered my knock, and I was glad to see that she didn't look unhappy to see me. I asked if I could come in.

"Sure." She stepped back from the door.

She had been wearing a black dress at the funeral, but she'd changed to jeans and a flannel shirt. She still looked good.

"I talked to Patrick Lytle at the cemetery this morning," I said. "I'd like to ask you about him."

She brushed her hair back with her right hand. "I thought that might be why you were here. I wish he hadn't shown up this morning."

"You told him about the service?"

"Yes. He asked me to call, so I did. I should have known better."

"Why did he want you to call him? Did he say?"

"He hated my father. He wanted to see him put in the mausoleum. That's all. And that's why I shouldn't have called him. No one should gloat at a funeral."

"Did you hate your father as much as Lytle did?"

"I told you the first time I saw you that my father didn't really mean much to me. I hardly ever saw him at all. I used to be bitter about that, and I guess I haven't gotten over it. If I had, I wouldn't have called Lytle."

"Your father bought you this place," I said, referring to the motel. "He must have had some feeling for you."

"If he felt anything it was probably just guilt. He thought that by buying me something like this he could make up for what he'd done to me and my mother, but he should have known he could never do that."

Maybe she was right about her father. I wasn't in a very good position to know Macklin's motives, but liked to think I could understand her feelings about him.

"Let's get back to Lytle's call," I said. "You told him that I was looking for Outside Harry, didn't you?"

She looked at me steadily with those deeply blue eyes. I couldn't see any guile or evasiveness in them.

"That's right," she said. "I did. Was there any reason I shouldn't have?"

I couldn't think of one. I hadn't told her it was a secret.

"No," I said. "Why did he call?"

"He'd heard about my father. He wanted to tell me to be sure to let him know when the funeral would be held."

"How did Harry's name happen to come up in the conversation?" I asked.

"I can't really remember. I think Mr. Lytle was asking me something about the investigation into my father's death. He wanted to know what the police were doing, and he asked if anyone else was looking into it."

"Didn't that strike you as curious?"

"Not really. And at the time I wasn't in much of a mood to wonder about it. I was wrapped up in my own problems. I was feeling a little guilty myself, if you must know. My father was dead, and I found I didn't really care very much."

I wasn't getting very far in my investigation, but that didn't matter to me at the moment. I was at least finding out that Cathy hadn't done anything wrong and that she didn't have any ulterior motive for having told Lytle that I was looking for Harry.

I felt an odd sense of relief. For a while there I had allowed myself to think that Cathy might even have had something to do with her father's murder. Looking at her now, and hearing her straightforward answers to my questions, I was sure that she was completely innocent of any involvement.

"I'll tell you what," I said. "Why don't you let me take you to dinner tonight. You could use a break. Call your friend Barbara and tell her to look after the place."

Cathy smiled. "You seem pretty sure she'll be willing to do that."

"Hey, you said she liked me."

"All right. I'll see. Call me later."

"You can count on it," I said.

Wally Zintner wasn't glad to see me. Neither was Dale Becker. They were crowded into Zintner's little office, probably going over their strategy for finding Harry.

"You locate him yet?" Zintner asked.

"No. Have you ever talked to Patrick Lytle about Harry?"

"Lytle? Hell, no. Dale and I are thinking of getting out of this whole damn mess. We've wasted too much time on it already. Let the dead bury their dead, I always say."

I'd never heard him say that, but that didn't mean he hadn't always said it to a lot of other people. It wasn't like Zintner just to drop something, though. He was a real bulldog when he got his teeth into something.

"What about your deal for The Retreat?" I asked.

"Hell, Smith, I wasn't cut out to be a big-time casino owner. I'll leave that stuff to Donald Trump and stick to what I know. I've got a pretty good business here."

"What about you, Dale?" I asked.

He gave me his best scowl. "I got nothin' to say to you."

That was just fine with me. And I thought I knew what was going on now.

"Minor got to you, didn't he?" I said.

Zintner started to deny it, then changed his mind.

"Got to *us*," he said. "I wasn't the whole show in this thing. There were other investors."

I took it that the "other investors" didn't refer to Becker. Zintner would never have cut Dale in on something as big as the deal for The Retreat.

"How much did Minor pay you?" I asked.

"Enough," Zintner said.

If he wasn't going to talk about it, that was all right with me. I'd already found out more than I'd hoped to. I knew now why Minor hadn't been following me. He'd been too busy working out a deal between Zintner and his principals. That didn't mean that Minor couldn't have killed Ro-Jo. It might even mean that he'd already found Harry.

"What about Harry?" I asked.

"We can't find him," Zintner said, and Becker nodded.

"And you don't care?"

"That was part of the deal," Zintner said. "Besides, I don't give a damn about Macklin now. I don't have any point to make with Minor. He and I are pals. So if Harry's got a secret, let him keep it."

"Just tell me one thing. Did Minor get Harry?"

Zintner's voice was flat. "He didn't say. I didn't ask. None of my business."

Becker nodded vigorously in agreement. He obviously didn't like the idea of having to deal with Minor. I wondered why.

"What about Ro-Jo?" I asked.

Zintner lit a Camel. Becker wrinkled his nose. He wasn't a smoker; I'd forgotten that he had one good quality.

"I don't know anything about Ro-Jo," Zintner said, a thin cloud of smoke floating in front of his eyes.

For some reason I didn't believe him. Maybe it was because he wasn't a very good liar. Dale was looking at the floor and fiddling with his earring.

I thought it was time to change the subject. "I want to get into some bank records," I said.

"That's illegal," Zintner told me, as if that was news. "Unless you've got a court order."

"Yeah," Becker said. "That's illegal."

I liked him better when he wasn't talking to me, but I didn't tell him that.

"Now that we all know it's illegal for me to get into the bank records, who do I talk to?" I said. "And forget the court order. I don't want to bring the police in on it. I need a name."

"Johnny Bates," Zintner said.

Another sign that I was slowing down. I should have thought of Johnny myself.

▽

28

KING VIDOR, SO I've been told, was a famous director in the early days of Hollywood, and for all I know it's true. You couldn't prove it by me, though. The only movie of his that I've ever seen was something called *Solomon and Sheba*, way back when I was a kid. It was made long after Vidor's glory days, and what I mainly remember is Gina Lollobrigida. She made quite an impression on me, but it wasn't a result of the way she took direction.

Anyway, Hollywood nostalgia aside, Vidor was born in Galveston, and his house is still here on the corner of 17th and Winnie. Johnny Bates lives less than a block away.

Bates is a strange guy, even for a city like Galveston, which has its share of strange guys. He's about my age, but he looks as if he went to sleep in 1968 and just woke up—shaggy black hair and beard, going gray now, with a hat to cover his bald spot, bell-bottom jeans, and usually a paisley shirt.

He was wearing one of the shirts when he came to the door. I don't know where he gets them. Maybe at the Goodwill outlet.

His latest toy was a flotation tank, which he showed me after inviting me in. The tank took up most of his living room.

"You really should try it out, Tru," he said. He grew up in Galveston, but he's lost most of his Texas accent. He spent a lot of time somewhere in the Northeast. "You just get in it and float."

Though Johnny said that the tank was made of fiberglass and lined with Styrofoam, the thing looked a lot like a coffin to me, and I didn't like it, especially not after having just seen Braddy Macklin laid to rest.

"I can float in the Gulf," I said.

"Not like this. No light, no sound, water exactly ninety-three point five degrees. There's nothing like it."

I couldn't disagree with that. "What about sanitation?"

"The water's salt water," he said, slapping the side of the tank with his hand. "There's nearly a thousand pounds of Epsom salts dissolved in there. Look at this." He pulled me around to the side. "Here's the filter and pump, and the water's purified by an ultraviolet process. No sanitation problems at all; I guarantee it. You could float a dead dog in there and then get in yourself without any risk."

A dead dog? "Sounds great," I said.

"It is. It really is. And you look like you could use it, if you don't mind my saying so. You look like you did after the game with Dickinson where you gained nearly two hundred yards before they decided to have the whole team maul you. Why don't you give the tank a try? You'll be so relaxed, you won't believe it."

He was absolutely right. There was no way I could believe lying in hot water in absolute darkness would relax me. I'd probably come out screaming in ten minutes. Or less.

"No thanks," I said. "I need your help with something else, though."

He looked disappointed that I wouldn't try his tank, but he was glad to help out. He told me that we should sit down and talk things over.

I didn't really want to sit down. Johnny was the only person I'd ever known who actually had beanbag chairs. But he flopped in one, so I fell into the other.

"So what's up?" he asked when he got comfortable.

"I need to look at some bank records," I said.

He didn't even blink. "Current?" he asked. "Or something older?"

"Both, I think."

"What's the bank?"

I told him that I didn't know. "But it's in Galveston. I'm pretty sure of that."

He shifted in the chair. I wondered if he was as uncomfortable as I was, but he probably wasn't.

"Not knowing the bank makes it a little tricker," he said, "but I can probably manage it. Whose records did you want to see?"

That was what I liked about Johnny. He got right to the point. No complaints about the difficulty of the job, no whining about legality or the impossibility of doing what I asked. And the main thing was that he would produce results. All he asked in return was that you didn't ask how he did it.

He'd been the same way for as long as I'd known him. In high school, if you wanted a copy of Friday's chemistry test, Johnny could get you one. If you needed tickets to see the Rolling Stones, Johnny could get them. If you parked in the wrong place in Houston and your car was impounded, Johnny could get it out. And it wouldn't cost you a cent. If you were his buddy, nothing ever cost you, not even the tickets to see the Stones.

He always insisted that you not inquire into his methods. As far as I know, no one ever did. Everyone was too happy with the results to care about how they were obtained.

Later in life, when Johnny went North, or so the stories went, he'd put his skills to work for various organizations on the shady side of the street and had made a lot of money doing it. Or possibly he'd worked for some super-secret government agency. It depended on who you talked to. All of that may have been legend, but no one ever asked Johnny about it. That was always part of the deal.

When he returned to Galveston, he had no visible means of support, but he lived very well indeed. I'd heard all sorts of rumors: that he was living off his ill-gotten gains; that he was running several 900 number hot lines that specialized in sex talk; that he was still working for the super-secret agency. I don't know that any of those things was true. Maybe they were all true. I didn't really care. All I wanted was information, and Johnny was the one who could get it if anyone could.

Among his many skills was his computer expertise. He was a hacker from way back, and I was pretty sure that with his equipment he could tap into the records of most any bank he wanted to. He got a new computer about every six months, never having been one to let technology get even a half step ahead of him.

Some of the records I wanted might not be on the bank's computer, however. They were probably too old.

"No problem," Johnny said, lifting his hat and running a hand over his bald spot. "They'll be on microfilm or fiche or something like that. All I have to do is locate the right bank. That'll take a little longer, but not much."

What he meant was that he'd have to get to the records in person, but I had no doubt that he could do it. If he chose to, he could look like a bank examiner or an oil millionaire from Odessa, depending on what the occasion demanded. And he had the credentials to go with the look. As the Texas expression has it, he cleaned up real good.

I told him what I wanted and asked how long he thought it would take.

"No doubt you wanted all this stuff about two hours ago," he said, settling his hat back on his head.

I admitted that he was right.

He sighed. "I wish just once somebody would come and ask me to get something they didn't need until next month."

"Never happen," I said. "Everybody's in a hurry these days. And by the way, Dino's paying."

Johnny's eyes lit up when I mentioned Dino. "Now *there's* somebody who'd appreciate my tank!"

"Don't even think it," I said.

"Hey, what're you talking about? Old Dino's been hiding out for so long that he'd be the perfect candidate." He gave the tank a fond look. "Can you think of a better way to withdraw from the world?"

I couldn't, of course. And that was just the trouble. Despite the fact that Dino had been doing much better lately, I was afraid that if he got into that tank, he might never come out.

"Forget it," I said. "Just do what I asked. OK?"

"You don't have to get pissy. If you want Dino to get out of the house, you should encourage him."

"I do. He and Evelyn have been out to see me a couple of times. I took him to eat at Shrimp and Stuff the other day."

"Get him to come over here. I won't even show him the tank. I promise."

I didn't see how he could avoid showing it to anyone, considering where it was sitting. Maybe he'd put a cloth over it and tell Dino it was some kind of altar to Poseidon. Anyone who knew Johnny would probably believe it.

"I'll try to get him over," I said. "But don't count on it."

"I won't."

He stood up with no trouble at all. I had to struggle.

"You're getting old, Tru," Johnny said.

"It's just that damn chair," I said.

He laughed. "Sure it is. Where are you going to be the rest of the day?"

I told him that I wasn't sure.

"Well, give me a call about five-thirty. If I'm going to find out anything, I'll know by then. And don't worry about having Dino pay me. This one's on the house."

"Dino has the money," I said.

"So do I. Don't sweat it."

That was fine with me.

I needed something to sit on top of Dino's chicken pot pie, so I went by McDonald's and got a quarter pounder with cheese, some fries, and a frozen yogurt. Yogurt is health food, isn't it?

Then I thought I might as well go home and read a few chapters of Thomas Wolfe while I waited for the news from Johnny Bates.

Going home was a mistake.

▽

29

I'D BEEN READING and listening to some CDs. Not Elvis this time. Leon Redbone. I'm a sucker for Leon Redbone, and I'm ashamed to admit what happened next. I went to sleep.

I don't usually sleep in the afternoons, especially when I'm listening to Leon. I suppose it was because I'd had a hard week, not to mention a mild concussion and several other bumps and abrasions. And then there were the drugs they'd given me in the hospital. Maybe it was the drugs. Or maybe it was the chicken pot pie.

Whatever it was, I was drowsing in the recliner with the book open on my lap. Nameless was asleep, too, but then Nameless is nearly always asleep. I've told him more than once that he's completely worthless as a watch cat, and he proved it again. He didn't even hear Alex Minor enter the house.

Of course I couldn't really blame Nameless. I didn't hear anything either.

I'm not sure what woke me up.

Maybe it was Minor looming over me.

Maybe it was Leon Redbone singing "Roll Along Kentucky Moon," which happens to be one of my particular favorites on the *Sugar* CD.

One thing was for sure; it wasn't Nameless who sounded the alarm. He was still sleeping soundly on the bed, one paw draped over his eyes.

I tried to sit up in the chair, but Minor reached out a hand as wide as the hardback copy of *Look Homeward, Angel* and just about as thick. He gave a little shove and pushed me back down.

He wasn't wearing his lawyer suit today. He was wearing jeans and a T-shirt that proved to me his muscles were just as big as I'd imagined they would be.

"I didn't hear the door," I said.

He smiled, which didn't improve his looks. "I didn't knock. You should try locking it."

Somehow I had a feeling that a lock wouldn't have stopped him.

"Nice music," he said. "Leon Redbone?"

"That's right. Are you a fan?"

"I have a couple of albums, but not that one."

"I could tape it for you." I thought about adding, "If you don't kill me," then thought better of it.

"Never mind," he said. "I'll pick it up one of these days." He pointed to the copy of *Look Homeward, Angel*. "How's the book?"

"You tell me."

"Underrated," he said. "People don't read Wolfe much these days, and professors don't like to teach him because he doesn't lend himself very well to the kind of highbrow analysis that Faulkner does, for example, but the son of a bitch could write."

Damn. I was sorry I'd said anything. He probably went to law school, too.

"I guess you didn't come here to discuss literature," I said.

"You guess right."

"So what did you come for?"

"I came because you don't strike me as the kind of man I can buy very easily."

I tried to sound greedy. "You never know until you try."

He didn't smile this time. "I know enough."

"Tell me something," I said. "Gerald Barnes didn't send you here the first time, did he?"

"Another good guess. This must be your lucky day."

Irony, yet. Minor had probably majored in literature. But I was sure that he had talents that he hadn't developed in his classes on literary devices.

"So it was Zintner," I said. "And good old Dale. Now there are a couple of guys you could buy."

He didn't bother to deny it. "They thought you might find Mercer before they could. Apparently they were wrong."

I didn't say anything. Maybe if he thought I'd found Harry, he'd go away.

He didn't go anywhere, however. He said, "I'm sorry about this, Smith. But it's business."

He reached behind his back for his pistol, and that's when I did what a judge should have done a long time ago.

I threw the book at him.

The corner hit him right above the left eye, opening a little cut and causing him to jerk his head to the right. I made an awkward jump out of the chair and tried to tackle him. It was like trying to tackle an oak tree. He hardly even moved.

I did, however, have his arms pinned to his sides, and he couldn't get to the pistol he'd been reaching for. He strained against me, and I knew I couldn't hold him like that for very long.

So I let him go.

He was so surprised that he almost fell. His arms flew out and up, and when they did I hit him in the gut with all I had. It was a little like hitting the sidewalk, but because he was already off balance, he stumbled backward.

I was sorry about what I did next, but I wasn't really thinking clearly at the time. I threw the CD player at him. The plug ripped out of the wall and the cord whipped along behind like a snaky black tail.

The player wasn't extremely heavy, probably not more than twenty-five pounds, but he wasn't able to get his arms up quickly enough, and it hit him pretty squarely in the middle of the forehead, opening up another cut and slamming his head back against the wall.

He hadn't been through as much as I had lately, so it didn't affect him as it would have me. If I'd been hit like that, I'd never have gotten up.

Minor did. Shaking his head and wiping his left hand across his face, he struggled to his feet, his right hand reaching for the pistol that I guessed was snugged in the small of his back.

While he was struggling, I was scrabbling on my closet shelf for the Mauser. It was still in the case, and I was glad that for once I'd broken a couple of my rules. I'd left the clip in the pistol.

I pulled the case off the shelf and got it unzipped just as a shot nearly deafened me and a slug tore off half the closet door frame.

Out of the corner of my eye I saw an orange blur as Nameless headed for more congenial surroundings. He was probably pissed that we'd waked him up. The fighting apparently hadn't bothered him, but the pistol shot was too much.

I grabbed the Mauser from the case, turned, dropped to one knee, and pulled the trigger. Minor was shooting, too, and the room was filled with the crashing of gunfire.

Under those circumstances, training and ability don't make much difference. What matters is luck, and I was luckier than Minor.

Maybe he was right; maybe it was my lucky day.

He shot the hell out of my wall and closet, but he missed me completely.

I, on the other hand, hit him twice, once in the right shoulder and once in the biceps. Fortunately he was right-handed, and my shots caused him to drop his pistol, which pretty much put him out of commission, considering that I was still holding onto mine.

The room was full of powder smoke, and the smell stung my nose. I walked over to Minor, who was leaning against the wall, and kicked his pistol under the bed. It was a nickel-plated Sig/Sauer .45.

"You owe me a CD player," I said. "And you probably made me ruin my Leon Redbone CD."

"Fuck that. Get me a doctor."

His shoulder was bleeding freely, though the arm didn't look so bad. Keeping the Mauser on him, I went to the closet and pulled out a towel. I threw it to him, and he caught it with his left hand.

"Hold that on it," I told him. "You'll be fine."

He pressed the towel to his shoulder. The blood started to soak it immediately.

"I need a doctor," he said. "This towel isn't worth a damn."

"It'll have to do until I'm through with you. As soon as we're through talking, I'll call 911."

"I don't have anything to say to you."

"Sure you do. For one thing, you can tell me who you're working for."

He considered it, but then he said, "I can't do that."

"You're going to jail for attempted murder if nothing else," I said. "And maybe the cops can even prove you killed Macklin and Ro-Jo. So you might as well talk."

"They can't prove what's not so," he said. "Call the number, dammit."

He could have been lying, but he was pretty convincing. "You didn't kill Macklin?"

"Hell no. Now get on that phone before I bleed to death."

I didn't think there was any danger of that. And besides, he was making me curious. So I didn't go for the phone.

"If you didn't kill Macklin, why were you looking for Harry?"

"Fuck you, Smith." He took a step forward. "If you don't make the call, I will."

"You take one more step, and I'll shoot your leg out from under you," I said.

I thought for a minute that he was going to try it, but he thought better of it and leaned back against the wall.

It was just as well. I don't know whether I could have shot him or not.

"Let's try it another way," I said. "I'll tell you something, and you tell me if I'm right."

He shrugged, which could have been either yes or no. He didn't look exactly eager to cooperate, however.

I gave it a try. "I think you're telling the truth about Macklin," I said. "You didn't kill him. Maybe you don't even know who did, and maybe you don't even care."

"You got that right," he said.

"You did kill Ro-Jo, though," I said. "I'm not sure the cops can prove it, but you did it."

He just looked at me, and I could see the answer in his eyes. He'd done it, all right. And after he still couldn't find Harry, he'd gone to Zintner and Becker and bought them off. Or threatened them off. Or maybe a little bit of both.

"I was wrong all along the line about you," I said. "Well, not exactly. I thought you might have killed Ro-Jo. I was right about that, but I was wrong about everything else."

"That's just too damn bad. Now are you going to call 911, or am I going to bleed all over your wall?"

"I'll call," I said. "I think I know all I need to know."

"You didn't get it from me," he said.

"No. You weren't any help at all. But that doesn't make much difference now. I've pretty much got things figured out."

"Maybe you're wrong again."

"Maybe," I said. But I didn't think so.

▽

30

NAMELESS DIDN'T SHOW up the whole time we were waiting for the ambulance. I suspected that he was behind the refrigerator, which was a place he'd hidden in the past, but I didn't have time to look for him. I had to keep an eye on Minor, who was feeling less and less perky thanks to his blood loss.

I figured that wherever Nameless was, he was fine. And he was probably asleep again. I didn't need to worry about him.

I did, however, have to worry about Gerald Barnes, which was my fault. I figured I might as well call him now and get it over with.

When he arrived, I admitted as little as possible. I told him that Minor had tried to kill me because I was looking for Harry Mercer, that I was sure Minor had killed Ro-Jo, and that Minor was probably involved in the murder of Macklin, though he might not have pulled the trigger.

"Can you prove any of this, Smith?" Barnes asked me.

I couldn't, of course. So I told Barnes that was his job. He didn't appreciate my attitude.

"I'd like to take you down to the jail and do some serious talking," he said, as if he missed the old days when he might have been able to use the rubber hose on me.

He had every right to feel that way, I suppose. He was the law, and I'd shot a man, after all. But this was Texas. I'd shot the man in my house, after all, where he'd come without an invitation. There wasn't a grand jury anywhere in the state that would return an indictment against me.

The case would go to the grand jury, no doubt about that,

but the D.A. would refer it without any charges; that was the way it usually went.

Barnes knew all that, but he didn't like it. He also didn't like the fact that because I had used my pistol on my own property, there was nothing he could do about it. I couldn't take the gun into town openly, but the law said I could use it in my own defense in my home.

So Barnes basically had to forget about me and be satisfied with Minor, who had already left the premises in the ambulance, under guard.

"You don't think he pulled the trigger on Macklin?" Barnes asked.

"You'll have to run a ballistics test to find that out," I said. "His gun's on the floor in my bedroom."

I really didn't have to tell him about the gun. He knew it already. He'd brought an investigative team with him, and they were going over the bedroom thoroughly while we talked.

"I'll be getting some other ballistics tests back pretty soon," Barnes said, referring to the one he was having run on the casings he'd found in the warehouse. "I'll probably be back to talk to you some more."

It was a pretty useless threat, I thought. He wasn't really going to be able to do much.

I said, "If you happen to find out that I fired my pistol in that warehouse, it really won't help you, will it? After all, Ro-Jo wasn't killed by a bullet. He was beaten to death. And Minor did it."

Knowing that I might be right didn't make Barnes any happier. He still wanted to charge me with something. And he thought I was still holding out on him.

That didn't hurt my feelings, however, because he was right.

It was well after five-thirty when I finally got rid of Barnes and his investigators. Barnes kept after me for as long as he could, trying to get me to admit some complicity in something that he could charge me with, but I didn't give him any satisfaction. He left, but I knew he'd be back.

As soon as he'd driven away, I called Johnny Bates.

"Hey, Tru," he said. "I was beginning to think you'd forgotten about me."

"No, I just had a visitor who didn't know when it was time to leave. Did you get what I asked for?"

"Sure I got it. What did you expect? You want the long version or the short one?"

I told him that I was in a hurry and that the short version would be fine.

"OK. Here it is: I saw the records, and you were right."

That was good news, but even the bank records wouldn't actually prove anything.

"Did you get copies?" I asked.

"Hey." He sounded hurt. "This is Johnny you're talking to. Of course I got copies."

"Great. Give me some of the specifics."

"Don't you want to come over and look at what I have for you?"

"I'll do that tomorrow. I need to know right now."

"All right. Here's the way it went."

He went on to explain that after locating the banks where Macklin and Lytle had accounts, he'd checked the deposits and withdrawals for both Patrick Lytle and Braddy Macklin. Beginning about the time Lytle's wife had disappeared, and continuing for years after, there were regular large withdrawals from Lytle's account. Just as regularly, there were large deposits in Macklin's account, almost always for exactly the same amounts that Lytle had withdrawn.

"Thanks, Johnny," I said, and meant it.

"It was easy," he said. "I just—"

"I'd love to hear all about it," I told him. "But let's make it tomorrow. I have something to do tonight, and it won't wait."

"All right, but when you come, bring Dino. I haven't seen him in just about forever."

"You get that tank out of the living room and I'll bring him," I said.

"I'll cover it up."

"I'll see you tomorrow, Johnny," I said. "And thanks."

"No sweat," Johnny said.

After he hung up, I called Cathy to tell her that I was going to be a little late but that we still had a date for dinner.

Then I called Patrick Lytle and told him that I was coming over.

It was after dark when I got to the old Lytle mansion. The oaks and magnolias looked even more impressive in the gloom of early evening. The darkness was kind to the old house as well, cloaking the fading paint and the weathered façade. There was only one light that I could see, and that was in the window of Patrick Lytle's room.

I got out of the Jeep and walked through thick shadows and up onto the dark porch. Paul Lytle answered the door again, and I followed him to his grandfather's room.

The old man was sitting silently in his wheelchair. He waited until Paul left the room to begin talking.

"I'm glad you called," he said. "I was hoping you might have some news for me. About Harry Mercer."

I shook my head. "It's not about Harry," I said.

"What, then?" he asked. "I'm not a man who likes to waste time, Mr. Smith."

"That's fine. I'm not either. So let me tell you what I know."

He wriggled around in his chair as if trying to find a comfortable position. His blanket slid off his legs, and I reached out to help him put it back.

He didn't thank me. "Please get on with it," he said.

I did. "Here's what I think happened. Your wife was having an affair with Braddy Macklin, and she divorced you because of it. I think your ego couldn't stand the shock, and I think you killed her for it."

I paused and watched him. There was no sound in the room except his wheezing breath.

A full minute passed without either of us saying a word.

Then I said, "I didn't expect you to admit it. However you did it, you must have done a good job. No hint of it ever got out. Everyone thought that she'd gone to Hollywood because she'd told friends that was what she'd like to do, but she never left town. You'd heard what she said, so you took advantage of the situation. You probably even packed her bags after you killed her. Maybe you buried them with her."

I thought about what Sally had told me, that she was sure Patrick Lytle hadn't buried his wife in the backyard. I wasn't so sure now that he hadn't.

Lytle didn't care what I thought, however. He was just sitting there, looking at me, listening attentively, his hands folded on his blanket.

"And do you have any proof of your wild speculations?" he asked.

"No. But there's more. I think you also killed Braddy Macklin."

"Now why would I do that?" He glanced down at his legs. "And *how* would I do it?"

"I don't know that part of it yet," I admitted. "But the why is easy. Braddy Macklin could have proved you killed your wife. Maybe he even thought about killing you in return, but he decided on something better. He decided to blackmail you. And I can prove that."

I told him about the bank records, which really proved nothing, though maybe he wouldn't realize it.

"There was something I'd been wondering about all along," I said. "How could Macklin afford to buy his daughter the Seawall Courts? That's some very expensive property, and even if the uncles paid Macklin better than I think they did for his bodyguarding services, he couldn't have afforded something like that motel. You could, however."

Lytle's mouth twisted with bitterness. "Yes, I could have afforded it. At one time. I'm very sorry to say that you're right, Mr. Smith. It was my money that bought that property. Braddy Macklin slowly bled me dry over the years, and he left me with only what you see around you—a decaying house. A useless body in a decaying house."

I didn't know much about the inheritance laws, but there was still a lot of money in Macklin's account. I supposed that Cathy was his only heir, but would the money be considered hers legally?

While I was wondering, Lytle was talking. "But you're wrong about one thing, Mr. Smith. I didn't kill Braddy Macklin."

"Who did?" I asked. "Alex Minor?"

Lytle was genuinely surprised. "What do you know about Alex?"

"Enough," I said. "I didn't know you two were friends."

"Not friends exactly," Lytle told me.

And then it all snapped together. "I'll be damned. Minor wasn't working for any syndicate back East. He was working for you."

Lytle looked regretful. "I really wish you hadn't reached that conclusion, though it is, of course, true. Or at least partially so."

"*You're* trying to buy The Retreat. You're not really opposed to gambling at all, not if you're the one making a profit from it."

"Sad but true. Gambling took everything from me. Everything. I thought it was time to see what it could give back."

"But what about the money?"

"I have . . . partners. In a way, you were right about Minor when you said he was from the East. He most certainly was. But the men for whom he worked didn't want to make a direct attempt to achieve a presence on the Island. They wanted a respected local, a man whose reputation was above reproach, to, as they put it, 'front for them.' I was the man they chose."

"Why you?"

He shrugged thin shoulders. "Who knows? I'm sure they did a great deal of research to discover just the right man. Certainly I need the money. I'm known to be rabidly opposed to gambling, but when the right moment arrives, I'll announce my conversion and say that I'm convinced gaming will be good for the Island if the right man is in charge."

"And the right man is you."

"Who could be better?"

I suppose he had a point there. "So you had Macklin killed not just because you hated him but because he was working for the opposition. Your reputation is really going to suffer on the Island after that gets out, Lytle."

"No one will find out about any of the sordid details. That is all in the past."

"The people here have awfully long memories," I reminded him. "And the police have Minor. He'll tell them what happened."

"Minor knows very little, Mr. Smith, and he won't tell about me."

"You can't be sure of that."

"No, I suppose that I can't, but I am convinced that Minor's masters are not the sort of men who would easily forgive him if he talked too much."

"He killed Macklin," I said, though I still found it hard to believe. He'd sounded so convincing. "The cops will get him for that, and he might talk to save himself."

"No," Lytle said. "He won't talk for that reason. A good attorney will get that charge dropped almost at once, even if it is made. You see, Minor did not kill Braddy Macklin."

I was getting confused. I thought I had things all figured out, but apparently I didn't.

"You've already told me that you didn't kill Macklin," I said. "And if you didn't, and Minor didn't, who did?"

"I did," Paul Lytle said from behind me.

I turned and saw him in the doorway. He had a .38 leveled at my chest.

Now I knew who'd been watching me from the window as I drove away on my first visit.

I was just sorry I hadn't figured it out sooner.

▽

31

PATRICK LYTLE SMILED. "Paul hated Braddy Macklin even more than I did."

"He stole from me," Paul explained. His voice was curiously toneless. "He took my inheritance. He took money that was rightfully mine, and he had to pay for that. I knew he had a key to The Retreat, and I called him about meeting there to discuss working for us. He didn't want to do that, but who cared? I shot him for what he did to me and my grandfather."

It was a nice little speech, and he probably believed most of it. Maybe he even believed all of it.

But I didn't. I was sure that his grandfather had planted the seed of revenge in his mind so that Paul would do what Patrick couldn't.

Not that it made any difference. Macklin was dead all the same, and he'd been killed by one of the Lytles.

"And Harry was there," I said. "He saw you kill Macklin."

"That was unfortunate," Paul said. "If he hadn't yelled out when I shot Macklin, I might never have known he was hiding there. He must have been somewhere in the back and come to see what was going on. I would never have thought he could get through that hole in the floor so quickly."

"He did, though," I said. "And he can still identify you."

"That is also unfortunate," Patrick said. "But we'll find him eventually. He doesn't seem exactly eager to go to the police, which is fine with us but too bad for him."

"If something happens to me, the cops are going to be very

suspicious," I said. "They know I was looking for Harry."

"And so does your client, I'm sure," Patrick said. "But suspicions really mean nothing. No one will be able to trace you to us."

"You're wrong about that," I said. "People know where I am."

Paul laughed. "I doubt that. But even if they do, it won't help you. We'll simply tell them that you were here, that you knew nothing of interest to us, and that you left."

"My Jeep's out front," I pointed out.

"I can drive," Paul said. "It won't be there long."

"He's wasting our time," Patrick told his grandson. "Kill him."

"In here?" Paul said.

The old man looked at his grandson with distaste. "No, of course not in here. Take him to the garage."

Paul stepped out of the room and motioned with the gun barrel for me to follow. I guess he thought that I would, though I couldn't imagine why he'd think I'd want to make things easy for him.

I wished I'd brought along the Mauser. If I'd had it, I would have tried to make things even more difficult for them, but the pistol was outside, under the front seat of the Jeep.

"I'm not going anywhere," I said, standing right where I'd been all along. "If you want to kill me, you'll have to do it here."

Patrick Lytle wheezed a sigh. "It would be messy. But Paul can clean it up. You might at least have a little dignity, Mr. Smith."

I didn't see anything dignified about dying in a garage as opposed to an old man's bedroom.

"Sorry," I said. "I'm just naturally uncooperative."

"Very well. Shoot him, Paul."

Paul might have shot Macklin, but that didn't make him a cold-blooded killer. He still had to take a deep breath before he pulled the trigger of the pistol.

When he breathed in, I dived for him.

He fired a shot that singed the top of my shoulder, and we both heard the unmistakable sound of a bullet hitting flesh.

Patrick Lytle gave a weak cry and began flopping around in his wheelchair just as I crashed into his grandson. The two of us hit the floor in a heap, and Paul shoved me aside, swinging the pistol at my head as he did so.

If he'd hit me, it would have been the end of things from my point of view, but I got my arm up in time to intercept the gun, which hit me right on the elbow. A sharp pain shot through my arm, and then the whole arm went numb. Paul jumped up and scooted for the door.

I was a little slower, and I took the time to look back at Patrick Lytle. He was leaning limply over the arm of the wheelchair, and he wasn't flopping anymore.

I didn't think that he'd be going anywhere, so I went after Paul.

I heard a door slam in the back of the house, but I wasn't going after Paul without a weapon.

So I ran to the front and went to the Jeep. By the time I had the Mauser out of the case, Paul was backing the van out of the garage.

I shot three times. The first one missed, but the next two hit the back tire on the driver's side. I put a couple of slugs into the other back tire just for good measure, and Paul brought the van to a stop.

He jumped out and started running toward the back of the house. I thought that there was probably a gate in the fence somewhere in that direction, though I didn't know where it was. Paul did, however. I had to catch up with him before he got to it, either that or shoot him. I didn't want to shoot him. I was afraid I might kill him. I'd been lucky with Minor, but I couldn't be sure my luck would hold.

I started running, hoping that my knee would hold up. And that I wouldn't run into a tree. I dodged the trunks as best I could, but the low-hanging branches kept swatting me in the face.

Paul kept running. The fence was about thirty yards away,

and I could see that I wasn't going to catch him before he got there. I was going to have to shoot.

I stopped and gripped the Mauser with both hands. I tried not to shake too hard. Firing a pistol after running is never a good idea. You might hit someone by accident.

My shot glanced off one of the concrete gateposts, which was what I'd intended, and it was close enough to Paul to throw a scare into him. He looked back over his shoulder, and that caused him to trip. He landed on his belly and skidded across the damp grass.

But he didn't drop the pistol. He was able to twist around and fire.

None of his shots came close. Falling affects accuracy even more than running.

Before he could get back to his feet, I caught up with him. He fired one more shot, which missed me by ten feet, and I kicked the pistol out of his hand.

He lay back on the ground and looked straight up at the night sky, his eyes blank.

"You can get up now," I said.

After a few seconds, he did.

We went back to the house, and I had Paul sit in the spindly chair in his grandfather's bedroom. I kept the pistol on him while I checked Patrick. There was a dark stain on his shirt, and it looked as if Paul had shot him right in the heart.

Paul didn't even look at the old man. He just sat quietly in the chair while I called the police.

▽

32

I MISSED MY date with Cathy that night, but I promised to make up for it later. She seemed to hope that I would. I didn't tell her that I'd caught up with her father's killer. That could come later too.

I didn't know what to tell her about her inheritance or about the way her father had obtained the money to buy Seawall Courts. I was sure that some of it would come out at Paul Lytle's trial, and Cathy could decide what to do then.

After the police finally got through with me, I went by Dino's house. Evelyn was there, and they were watching "Nightline." They turned it off to hear my story, which took a while.

After I finished telling it, Dino asked me about Harry.

"I haven't found him," I said.

"But don't you think he's all right?" Evelyn asked.

"He probably is. No one was able to find him through this whole thing. This is a small island, but there are plenty of places to hide. Harry's all right."

Dino wasn't so sure. "I hope you know what you're talking about."

So did I.

Jody called me the next day, very early. I was reading the newspaper when the phone rang. Nameless, who had come out of hiding, was asleep on my bed.

"You still lookin' for Harry?" Jody asked.

I said that I was.

"Miz Williams say to tell you where he is. She told him that the man who kill Mr. Macklin in the jail now, but Harry don't believe her. He say he won't come out till he talk to you."

"I'll talk to him," I said. "Where is he?"

Jody gave me the address. "I better go with you," he said.

That was fine with me.

Harry was in a vacant apartment in the housing project near where Mrs. Williams lived. Jody guided me to it without any trouble, and I got the impression that he'd been there before. I didn't ask him, however. I was just glad to have him with me. It cut down on the number of suspicious looks I got, though not by many.

The room was full of things that Harry had brought with him, and there was a strong smell of what I hoped was tuna and not canned cat food. I thought about the cats that lived in the rocks along the seawall. They would have loved Harry.

Harry seemed glad to see me. The first thing he wanted to know was whether the man who'd shot Macklin was really in jail. I told him that it was true.

"Tha's good," he said. "I didn' like that man. He point that gun at me, and I scoot right back out that hole."

"You should have gone to the police, Harry," I said.

He looked at me as if I'd lost my mind. "Who gonna b'lieve a crazy ole man like me?"

"I would," I said. "So would the police."

"Po-lice don't think much of me," Harry said. "I don't like 'em. 'Sides, I never saw that man in my life. I didn' know who he was."

And that was that. I knew he'd never tell Barnes or any other cop what he'd seen. That wouldn't keep Paul Lytle out of prison, however. My testimony should take care of that.

"Are you ready to get out of here?" I asked Harry.

"You got that right," he said. "I flat tired of bein' cooped up like a chicken. I need to get out where I can *breathe*."

"Get your stuff together, then," I said. "Nobody's after you anymore."

Harry laughed. "Tha's good," he said. "Tha's real good."

He was obviously quite happy, but he didn't feel any better than I did.

I had another couple of stops to make after Harry was out of the apartment and back on the streets.

Sally West was almost as glad to see me as Harry had been. She'd heard the news about Lytle on the radio and she wanted the straight scoop.

She sipped Mogen David while I told her the whole story. It was just too early for me to drink, but Sally didn't seem to mind.

When I'd finished talking, she said, "Do you really think the police will find Laurel Lytle under the floor of the garage?"

"It's a dirt floor," I said. "That's probably where they were going to put me, so I figured maybe Lytle had used it before."

"You should be proud of yourself, Truman," she said.

"Why's that?"

"Because you found Harry. Because you kept anything from happening to him."

"I got lucky," I said.

She looked at the glass that held her wine. "There's more to it than that. You 'got lucky,' as you put it, because you cared enough about an old man to try to help him. Not everyone would have done that."

Maybe not, but I was just glad that even if I hadn't found Harry until his friends decided it was safe for him to come out, I'd at least gotten in the way of everyone else who was after him, and in doing so maybe I'd kept him alive. It didn't make up for not finding Jan until it was too late, but it helped.

"Thanks," I told Sally. "I'm glad you think I did something right."

"I'm the one who should thank you," she said. "You make me feel almost young."

Hearing that cheered me up almost as much as finding Harry had.

* * *

Dino was next.

"How much do I owe you?" he asked, taking the sack of Big Red that I handed him.

"Whatever you gave me to begin with was enough," I said. "You want to go see Johnny Bates this afternoon?"

"Johnny Bates? I haven't thought about him in a long time. What's he got to do with this?"

"He helped me out on a few things. Put some of that Big Red on ice and I'll tell you all about it."

"Yeah. I'll do that. And maybe I'll even go see Johnny with you."

He turned to go to the kitchen, but I stopped him. "Do you have a fishing rod?" I asked.

"Never owned one in my life," he said.

"That's all right. I have three or four. You can borrow one."

"Why would I want to do that?"

"Because after we go by Johnny's place, we're going fishing."

Dino looked hesitant. "I don't know about that."

"You'll love it," I assured him. "We'll stop by Jody's and buy some shrimp. We can get some salt pork, too."

"Salt pork?"

"If the fish aren't biting, we'll tie some bacon on a string and go crabbing."

Dino smiled. "I haven't been crabbing since I was a kid."

"It's about time, then," I said.

"Yeah," Dino said. "I guess it is."